TO THE DEVIL

TO THE DEVIL

William Jack

Robin Clark · London

First published in 1988 by Robin Clark Ltd
A member of the Namara Group
27/29 Goodge Street
London W1P 1FD

Copyright © 1988 William F. Jack

British Library Cataloguing in Publication Data
Jack, William F., *1945–*
 To the devil.
 I. Title
 813'54[F]

ISBN 0-86072-110-8

Typeset by MC Typeset Limited, Chatham, Kent
Printed and bound in Great Britain
at The Camelot Press plc, Southampton

For Olga and Nina, in memory.

Note

This manuscript was found in December 1986, in the bottom of an empty vegetable crate behind the service entrance of the American Embassy on Kalinin Prospekt in Moscow.

The fry cook who found it called the chef who, thinking it was a secret document drop, called for the marine corps security guard.

The document, now called 'Anonymous Dispatch C–23', was translated painstakingly at CIA headquarters in Langley, Virginia. The chief translator's report noted that there were strange markings on the pages, and that partially eaten cabbage leaves lay between the pages of the manuscript.

In an attempt to identify the author, an analysis was performed on the typeface. It was determined that the manuscript had been typed on a Smith-Corona manual office typewriter. The letters suggest that the machine was modified for Russian-language typing somewhere between the Great Soviet People's Alphabet Reform of 1918 and the Great Soviet People's Alphabet Reform of 1921. The typist (presumed to be the author) frequently interpolated the letters 'e' and 'i', suggesting he or she was of Ukrainian origin. It is obvious that the author was a bad typist and, in general, had sloppy work habits.

The manuscript was declassified from 'top secret' to 'for

anyone who wants it' after it was decided that the story had no meaning – direct, indirect, hidden or otherwise. Michael Flurffy, chief translator on the project, resigned in protest, claiming a devious message lay hidden between the lines.

Guardian of the public morals Reverend Bobby Jim Jerwell agreed, and columnist Tom Callous wrote a piece called 'Ezekiel's Prophecy Comes True: The Scourge of the Big Northern Bear'. Evangelist Tommy Swagger read portions of the work on Sunday mornings on national television, but refused to identify the title or source of 'the devil's own filth' from which he read. Highly placed personnel in the FBI likewise considered it an encoded message to terrorists and conspirators.

This edition is the first publication of the full text.

One

The world would never be the same. Things started to turn strange at the Tikvin Biomedical Research Centre in October, late October. No, September. Mornings had started out as they always had. The phones weren't working, and the 'out of order' sign still hung on the elevator door. The cursed French! Their elevator had never worked.

Every time the engineers came from their office in Paris or Madrid or some other place in France, they complained about the food (it wasn't subtle enough, they said), and about the way Soviet workers had installed the elevator (also not subtle enough).

'The shaft – she is crooked,' their shifty-looking interpreter said, his crooked, perverted eyes fixed on the walls. Everyone knows a shaft is a 'he'.

Pantemelion Pantemelionovich, the Moscow building inspector, tried to look important in front of the foreigners. He called in the architects, along with the builder (who was vacationing in Yalta with his mistress), the contractor (who was in a prison of his own construction, for taking bribes) and trade-union officials (who were not in prison, but should have been).

All of them pointed to the blueprints, which called for a straight shaft. So a straight shaft it was, they declared – to hell with the Frenchmen's accusations. The foreigners didn't even know Russian, probably couldn't read blueprints anyway. If the plans called for a straight shaft, then a straight shaft it was. Shirking responsibility, the greasy Napoleons.

'But see, she is crooked!' the long-nosed foreign interpreter repeated in twisted Russian, as if he'd discovered a new continent. It wasn't news. The croissant-eater could hardly take credit. The whole building was crooked – the stairs, the windows, the floors. The walls buckled in the middle, so from the outside the place looked like a three-storey beer barrel.

Inside was worse. People got headaches. Cockroaches bumped into one another. It had been that way before the revolution, when some merchant or other lived there. It had been that way during Lenin, during Stalin, during Khrushchev and Brezhnev and the ones who came later.

'They should go back to France, back to eating their goose eggs,' Nikita the janitor declared, shaking his head. Nikita had worked in the building for so long that he himself was crooked, one shoulder higher than the other, one arm longer to compensate and two beady eyes slanting off in opposite directions.

Who would have known that this was the beginning of the end, or nearly so; that the world would never be the same again?

Two

So the Frenchmen left the workers' paradise, and things went back to normal, or nearly normal, at the barrel-shaped Tikvin Institute.

Then the phones started to work, the first time in years. They rang off the hook. When answered, there was a click.

Then silence. The sound of bells was an evil omen.

Lydia Ivanovna leaned back in her chair, picking her teeth with a ruler. It was a Western ruler, much thinner that the sturdy Soviet kind, just the right size for getting between molars. When the phones rang, she whacked them with the ruler, like misbehaving children. Sometimes she stuck the bent ruler in under the receiver and flipped it like a sausage on a griddle, the thing flying off in the air, stunning itself by banging into the side of the desk, then hanging unconscious, dangling from its noose.

Lydia was not a kind or subtle person. None of the Frenchmen tried to get inside her skirts (there was room enough for all of them – their wives too, the immoral captalists). They chased every other skirt in town; the Russian women dropped like flies. Show them a skinny neck, smile a puckered, pukey smile, swallow half the sounds in the Russian mother tongue, and the ladies fall, the immoral swine! The devil take them all!

While Lydia Ivanovna picked her teeth and didn't answer the phones, Sofinya Haroldovna (the lord knows how she acquired such a name; mortals shouldn't pry into other people's business) typed, or didn't type. A black Smit-Korona sat like a fat mechanical cat on her desk, making a racket when she clawed at it, which was seldom. She read novels or poetry, marking her place with a fat pencil from the Frederick Engels Pencil Factory Number Five (stolen probably) when it was time for productive labour. She tapped with one finger on the machine, said 'Damn!' or 'The devil!' and went back to her novels.

The world would never be the same. Lydia would never be the same either, but in a different way. She was as thin as a bird when they hired her, got fat later. Sofinya would never be the same either. The name 'Haroldovna' had intrigued the personnel officer, who had a weakness for Spanish music. By the time they found out she couldn't type, Nikolai Semyonovich, the former director, had taken a liking to her. Then he was transferred, first to the Odessa prison, then to the Odessa opera. It was a demotion. No one listened to him, as they had in the prison.

Petrushenko, the current director, decided to keep her anyway. 'The name lends a certain aura to the institute,' he announced. Sofinya's typing, or not typing, didn't slow things down anyway. That was the beauty of the Tikvin Institute. No official correspondence came in. The postman hardly stopped at 34 Bashmakovsky Prospekt. When the phones rang, it was usually a wrong number, someone screwing up in the central switchboard office, or Misha the poet calling for Sofinya, his mother. Pity the poor typist – a poet for a son. Or he said he was a poet. No job. No publications since high school. Not even a member of the writers' union. Sofinya stole stationery for him. Imagine Pushkin writing a sonnet on the back of a letterhead of an institute that didn't exist. A parasite, not a poet.

Three

An institute that doesn't exist? The institute existed on paper, by plan only.

Moscow had been short on institutes, per capita, in the 1950s. It looked bad for the tourists. Long on spats factories (which is what the building contained, after the revolution). Spats went out of fashion in the 1920s. The factory fell out of existence during the sixth year of the five-year plan in 1952, just at the time they were short on institutes. The shaft went in (or down) in 1964. The Frenchmen brought in their elevator in 1972. The professor came in 1982. Nikita, the janitor, wore spats, probably the only person in Moscow. The professor wore felt boots in the winter, slippers in the summer. He didn't pay attention to anything, not even to Lydia when she was thin, or Sofinya when she was pretty.

Lydia let herself go, as they say, but the expression hardly fits. She let all of herself stay – all two hundred pounds of her, adding a kilo or two a week, coming to work in the morning with a sack of food, leaving at night with the sack empty, her legs pushing her skirt further out to the sides. Papers that crossed her desk had blueberry stains in the spring, ice-cream stains in the summer, and chocolate marks all year round.

It had been an easy ten years at the Tikvin Institute. No plans to meet or quotas to fulfil. No speeches on a glorious mission (there was none), no budget meetings, no bureau inspectors. The institute had no goals, so it never failed to reach them. No one had to worry about losing funding. When you don't make mistakes, no one takes your money or job away. Section chiefs and party watchdogs, lab attendants and clerical staff – they all walked around with smug smiles on their faces, winking at one another.

So it was a normal day, Tuesday. Sofinya sat at her desk, puffing a cigarette, while Lydia waved her fat arms, fanning the smoke towards the window. The sounds of snoring, regular and peaceful, came from behind Petrushenko's door, where the 'In conference' sign hung crooked on a nail. A long snort, then silence, followed by a whistle, all in a regular rhythm. It was reassuring.

'Holy lord! God save us all!' Nikita limped into the room, his crooked eyes wide with excitement. As if he'd seen the devil himself. 'A black Chaika!' he moaned, pointing towards the doorway with his crooked broomstick shaking in the air.

'You drinking?' Lydia looked up at him with her beady eyes. 'You see black seagulls in Moscow?'

'To hell, woman! A Chaika! A black Chaika! Not a bird

– the car!'

'A car? So what?' She bit into a pirozhok, rubbing her fingers on a piece of paper lying on top of the stack on her desk. 'You're drinking again, Nikita. I'll call your wife. She'll drag you out of here by the ear, like on revolution day.'

'A Chaika, woman! An official car! Snooping! Driving right up Bashmakovsky!'

'It's going somewhere else! So what?'

'It's coming here! Bashmakovsky's a dead-end street, woman!'

'So what?'

'Curtains on the back windows!' Nikita spoke ominously, the broom handle shaking in his hand. 'A driver in a leather coat! KGB!'

'Holy mother! God save us!' It was Lydia's turn to shake, and shake she did, her arms flailing in the air, rolls of flab waving in the wind. You could almost see drops of sweat flying off her red forehead. 'Inspectors! We're done for now!'

Her hands ran through the stacks of papers on her desk, and dust clouds rose. 'Inspectors! A black day for us all! A black day!'

Four

'The devil! What can we do? The devil!' Lydia Ivanovna wailed, pulling on her cheeks with her fat fingers.

The front door slammed. Footsteps coming down the hall. Deliberate, even footsteps. Not Nikita's crooked shuffle or the professor's tiny-footed patter. An omen. Getting louder, like a ticking clock. A German time bomb.

'Security,' said a tall, skinny man with beady eyes, a

hooked nose, and a sour expression on his face. Sizing up the place as if he'd move in tomorrow. A leather coat that fitted so well it looked as if it was made just for him.

'State security,' he repeated, flicking open his lapel, showing the dreaded red button pinned inside.

'We haven't – I – I – haven't done – anything,' Lydia stammered, wedging herself upwards by pressing her fat arms on to the desk top. 'I haven't done anything!' she repeated, beating her breasts. It was true.

'Ivan Flaffanoff, special division.' The tall man grinned a sinister grin with his puffy lips. He was holding an official-looking pass between his big-knuckled fingers, right in front of Lydia's eyes. 'Special security,' he added, emphasizing the word 'special'.

'Oh lord! Oh lord!' Lydia gasped and pounded her breasts. She swung sideways, and her chair ran off, wheels squeeking, across the crooked floor, banging up against the side of a filing-cabinet. The top drawer flopped open like the mouth of a gaping peasant, and a tongue of brown, wrinkled folders with black finger-marks licked towards the KGB agent.

'Boris Borisovich Proplavsky.' The tall man broke the silence, rubbing his finger alongside his nose. 'We're looking for Professor Proplavsky.'

'Oh, the professor!' Lydia sounded relieved. 'It's the professor! Not us! The professor!' she announced, sweeping her arms around the room. 'He's up on the third floor – in his laboratory.'

She wiped her forehead with a crumpled paper, snuffed out the cigarette still smoking in Sofinya's ashtray, then licked her finger. 'Three floors up. We don't know anything about him – what he does, when he comes and goes. We don't know anything.'

'How do I get to his laboratory?' Flaffanoff, the tall man, asked with impatience.

'I don't know,' she said, shaking her head. 'I've never been up there, you see,' she added, as if on trial. 'It's somewhere up the stairs. The elevator doesn't work – I know that much – they told me it doesn't work – I've never been in it – never been up there, you see. Never!' She crossed herself twice.

Three more men walked in and took their places behind Flaffanoff – all looking off in different directions with one shifty eye, their other eye on Lydia.

'The stairway's over there,' Lydia said, pointing back out to the hallway. 'The laboratory – it's up there, up the stairs. This is an office, not a laboratory.' She shuffled through the papers on her desk. 'An office.' She gestured towards the papers. 'We answer phones. They never ring. We answer correspondence. We never get any.' She caught herself in mid-sentence. 'We work. We are a productive office.'

Sofinya had quietly tucked away her novel and turned to her typing. Click. Click. Click. Ring. Click. The sounds of her Smit-Korona filled the room. The bell was an evil omen.

Things would never be the same, not in the office, not with the professor, not anywhere.

Five

Who would have been interested in Professor Boris Proplavsky? Why would an official black Chaika have headed up dead-end Bashmakovsky for the likes of him?

The professor hardly existed, at least in any official sense. After the Tikvin Institute had fallen through the cracks in the plan, after its first three projects had been terminated – the first for deviating from the path of the people, the second for deviating from the path of the party, the third for just deviating – the scientists and professors abandoned ship, slinking out under cover of darkness, research notes and equipment hidden under their lab coats.

An easy job hadn't been worth the risk. The Tikvin Institute for the Study of Social Behaviour. The title alone was enough to scare anyone. Too bourgeois, too capitalistic, too decadent. A person could get a one-way ticket to Krasnoyarsk for working on things like that. Sociologists. They're lower than parasites, loafers and shirkers of duty. Tikvin himself had been a sociologist, it was rumoured. Thrown into prison three times, rehabilitated twice. Dinner with Comrade Stalin one evening, a train ride to the Far East the next day. Sociology was a risky business, worthy of a trip to Kamchatka when the political winds changed.

So the other scientists left, like rats from a sinking ship, slinking out the back doorway. The institute became a Biomedical Research Centre.

Only Professor Proplavsky had remained, shuffling in late in the morning, working until late at night, smiling and humming to himself. He wore a long coat over his frock in the winter. You could hardly see his feet. Little feet, they were. He took small steps that pattered across the floor, his legs spinning fast, in a fury, like a paddlewheel steamer. But the old boat hardly moved, and hardly talked. 'Morning,' is all he said. Not even 'good morning'. Just 'morning'.

A mysterious person. Too quiet. Letters came from foreign countries, with puny-looking stamps – a skinny queen with a sour smile, old men with puckered faces and powdered wigs. Maybe that's why he was under suspicion. Correspondence with foreign interventionists.

The professor hardly ever came down from the laboratory, never bothered anybody. A mysterious, quiet type, just the sort to fall under suspicion. And no wonder.

Two or three years ago, crates with holes cut into their sides started arriving from collective farms. Ducks. Geese. Quack. Honk. Their sounds and their smells filled the halls and the office. Nikita complained of goose shit, and a fat crooked-necked goose followed him around, pecking away at his backside. Ducks plopped down the stairway, quacked and strutted into the office, staring at Sofinya's typewriter. Geese held court in the stairwell, grumbling or honking the afternoon away, picking at cockroaches.

The ducks had disappeared into the cellar when Flaffanoff and his crew had entered the institute. Ducks are smart.

Six

The fateful meeting between Flaffanoff the security agent and Proplavsky the professor would have been lost for the masses and the ages, had it not been for Petrushenko. He had been sound asleep when the commotion started. Comrade Security Agent Flaffanoff had frowned at the wheezing and snorting coming from behind the director's door. Then the snoring had stopped, but the door didn't open. Petrushenko's fat nose stuck out from his doorway only after Flaffanoff had gone upstairs.

'Architects again?' Petrushenko asked Lydia Ivanovna.
'Worse!'
'Building inspectors?'
'KGB!' Lydia humphed.
'Oh lord – the devil!' Petrushenko gasped, as if unable to make up his mind.

Petrushenko was a clever man. Lazy, but clever. He'd

worked in the Ukraina Hotel before transferring to the institute. He'd been manager of guests' comfort, surveillance and security there. He'd set up a system of listening devices and peeping holes throughout the hotel, keeping up on state secrets. He was fired when they found out he spent most of his time listening in on newlyweds or peeking into shower stalls. There were rumours. Some said he peeked at boys. Others said he peeked at the ladies. He was transferred right into non-existence, to the barrel-shaped Tikvin Institute on dead-end Bashmakovsky.

'Why is it called Bashmakovsky Prospekt?' had been his first question. 'It's not a prospect. It's hardly a pereulok, not even an alley!'

Because of his hotel expertise (at surveillance, not at peeking), he'd improved the institute's own security system, planting listening devices all over the place. They were so obvious no one talked around them. One hung over the toilet cistern, next to the chain, for instance. Another was stuck behind a radiator, until winter, that is, when it turned a sickly shape and drooped down towards the floor.

Petrushenko, still coughing up phlegm as he did every time he woke up, opened the secret doors in his anteroom, exposing the innards of his listening machine. His head rested sideways up against a dusty oval speaker, and his bony hands caressed the round, greasy knobs.

'I've got them now – the laboratory!' he said proudly, winking towards Lydia Ivanovna.

Plop. Scrape. Flush! Disgusting. 'Wrong outlet,' he said shyly, spinning the knobs.

'Comrade Proplavsky.' It was the right knob. Flaffanoff's voice. 'Your work, your discoveries – they may have applications – helpful applications.'

Quack. Quack. It was the ducks in the laboratory.

Honk. Honk. It was the geese.

'Applications? This is theoretical science. What do you mean by applications?' The gravelly voice was the professor's. The tone said he didn't respect his visitors enough. Maybe Flaffanoff hadn't shown him the red pin.

'Applications,' Flaffanoff repeated. 'To people.'

'To people?' The professor spoke in a mocking tone. 'A duck that honks. A goose that quacks. You would find applications to people?'

'This may be a discovery of major importance – it could change the nature of our operations.'

Quack. Quack. Honk. Honk. The rest of the conversation was drowned out, lost to posterity.

Seven

They helped Professor Proplavsky down the stairs and out to the hall. That's the polite way to put it. It could be said they carried him out of the building, Flaffanoff coaxing him from the right, and one of his henchmen from the left, the professor's feet taking their little customary steps, this time flapping a half-metre off the ground.

Lydia Ivanovna breathed a sigh of relief and went back to her eating, promising never again to let any foreign letters pass across her desk. 'Evil things come of it – look at the professor!' she said, between bites on her greasy pirozhok.

Then two weeks later the professor was back in the institute, quietly working as usual, except that there were agents fawning all over him, offering him tea, coffee even. Where would they get coffee? In all of Moscow there was none, but these lackeys found it somewhere, maybe by travelling across borders.

Flaffanoff stepped into Petrushenko's office one morning and, in a voice of authority seldom heard by anyone in the institute, announced, 'Whatever the professor wants – whatever he needs, you give him.' Flaffanoff's ears wiggled as he spoke. 'If you cannot obtain it, contact us.'

Lydia was amazed. She'd try it. 'The professor loves meat pies – pirozhki stuffed with lean beef.'

It was a lie, but a test. She knew there was little beef, much less lean beef, to be had that week in Moscow. Twenty minutes later, Lydia munched on a meat pie with a filling leaner and sweeter than any she'd ever had. Even the crust was done just right, not raw in the middle, not burnt around the edges.

'Such a pirozhok!' she exclaimed, pinching it tenderly with her fat fingers. 'A prize of Soviet workmanship!' She took a big chomp right out of the middle. 'Quality of the first magnitude!'

'Move over, woman!' Her amazement turned to scorn. Boryachka, Flaffanoff's skinny assistant, was tugging at her chair-back. 'I need to sit here too, by the phones. Move over!'

'You faggot! You bony, snivelling pederast!' She punched him with her pirozhok, this one filled with cabbage. 'I've worked here fourteen years, always with my chair in this very spot! Look! There are worn spots in the floor from the casters! There!'

'Move over, you hefty old hag! You're under surveillance now – a part of the plan! I'll answer the phones now.' He grabbed at the phone, sticking his finger daintily into the receiver.

'That's my job – my phone!' Lydia grabbed at the base. Boryachka let out a squeal as his twisting finger followed her grab.

'Ow! It's not your phone!' Boryachka squealed.

'It is!'

'It's state property!' With that, Boryachka worked his finger free and stuck it into his mouth. 'You brazen hussy! You – you vamp!'

The phone tipped over in the struggle. The receiver swung, like a hanged man, off the side of the desk, banging up against the metal. It was an abuse of state property, a crime for which a servant of the state could be punished severely.

'Now look what you've done, you gomo!' Lydia pointed to the swinging receiver. 'You – you've upset communications – state communications! That's a crime too!'

'Move your rump, fatty! I'll tell Flaffanoff!'

Boryachka stood, hissing and lisping, and Lydia sat, huffing and cursing under her breath – each pushing into the other. They did not get along very well.

Eight

'Kvak. Kvak.'

'Not good. Try again, Vasenka.'

'Koo-ack. Koo-ack.'

'Better. Still terrible. Come, Vasenka. Let us dine. Then we'll try some more.'

Arnold the duck was about to give up. Vasenka, his Russian pupil, couldn't get the hang of it.

'If you're going to America, you must pass yourself off as an American duck. Try again. Quack. Quack.'

'Kvak. Kvak.'

The other ducks laughed.

'The rest of you – keep kviet – I mean, quiet!' It was hard enough speaking two duck languages without all the kvaking in the cages. It echoed down the institute corridors. Not by any means an atmosphere conducive to learning new languages.

Arnold was a foreigner, and acted like it. Strutted like a goose. Held his beak too high in the air. Picked at his food too much. In short, the product of a pampered Western life.

When the professor had requested an American duck, Arnold had been flown in on a special Aeroflot plane from Kansas via Montreal. He sat on a seat in the first-class section, puffing on a Cuban cigar. A sophisticated duck.

'Destination: Moscow Zoo,' his travel papers had said, and he was whisked right through customs and passport control. They didn't even inspect his luggage. The soldier in the customs booth didn't spend ten minutes looking at him, then at his picture, then at him, as he did with all the other foreign visitors. Little did anyone know that Arnold was part of something that would change the world.

'For the plan to work, I need an American duck,' the professor had explained. He wouldn't tell why.

'Believe me, I need an American-born duck,' he repeated. Flaffanoff listened, and the wheels of bureaucracy churned until they spat out an Arnold, coming in on a flight from Montreal.

He'd arrived in a white plastic cage with rounded corners, exhausted from travel and jet-lag – worse than any tourist. But two days later he was up and around, having his way with the institute, poking at all its nooks and crannies, wadling down its corridors, his Soviet compatriots close at his webbed feet, pointing out the amenities (there were few).

The Soviet ducks avoided Arnold at first. They considered him stuck-up. Aloof. An individualist. A queer quack. In short, pampered in a way no Soviet duck could imagine. Then special sacks of feed started finding their way to the Tikvin Institute via special KGB courier from the Ukraine. Cultural barriers broke down. Arnold became a benefactor, then a friend.

Vasenka was the most compliant, intellectually curious Soviet duck, so it was natural he was chosen as Arnold's protégé, his right-hand duck. The professor looked on with favour as Arnold and Vasenka conversed during their long walks, as they became more and more friendly. There were rumours that the pair of ducks had become too friendly. Vasenka, after all, had Belorussian connections.

'You look very handsome this morning, Vasenka,' Arnold would say in his foreign accent.

'And you too, you too,' Vasenka would reply, as they waddled together down the corridor, the professor following, bent low, writing as he walked, his little feet skipping under him.

Nine

The sign over the doorway of the Tikvin Institute still said, 'Closed temporarily for renovation.' Rust marks from the nails ate into the metal.

Petrushenko stood high on a ladder, shoving a large camera into an aperture, and trying to jam shut the door.

'How will it take pictures if the door is shut?' Lydia Ivanovna asked, between licks on her 'Polar Ecstasy' ice-cream bar.

'It doesn't matter. We're out of film anyway.' He seemed annoyed by the question.

Quack. A duck waddled across the floor, almost tipping the ladder.

'Damn ducks! To the devil with them all!' Petrushenko waved his hands in the air until the ladder started to totter, then crossed himself and held on to its sides.

'Then why install the camera?' Lydia Ivanovna asked,

pointing towards the camera with her second ice-cream bar, 'Northern Lights', covered with chocolate.

'That's my job, woman.'

'Then why not get film?'

'That's not my job.' He looked at her as if she were stupid. She was. 'It's someone else's problem – not mine. Not yours either.'

'Hmpff!' Lydia clawed at the newspaper wrapped around her meat pie. The crust was so juicy, the paper transparent. The newsprint ended up stamped on to the crust, in reverse order. nagrO ytraP laiciffO.

It was hard to have a leisurely lunch. Things had never gone back to normal since the professor returned with Flaffanoff.

The professor's laboratory now occupied the entire third floor. Ducks and geese honked and quacked in the hallways. They took over the building, walked where they pleased, shat where they pleased.

'Goose shit! I hate it!' old Nikita said, scowling and sweeping away with his broom. 'It eats right through my broom bristles! You know how long it takes to requisition a broom?'

No one answered. No one cared how long it took to requisition a broom.

'Oy! The smell curls the hair in my nose,' he said, bending down to scrape away at a hardened little pile in the doorway. Ivanushka the goose bent his long neck into a weird contortion and peered into Nikita's nose. It was true, was true.

It was not good to complain. The institute was filled with agents. Plain-clothes agents, but agents all the same. Not plain clothes. Clothes too typical to be plain or ordinary. Fat men dressed as students in levi djinzy that didn't fit. Chubby lady agents cursing the tight skirts that wouldn't let them bend or stoop to peer under doorways. Pimply young spies dressed like workmen, turning their stuck-up snouts away from their proletarian garb, peeking over the tops of their shovels. Old ladies sweeping spaces they'd already swept, stepping over piles of goose droppings. When a stranger walked up that part of Bashmakovsky street, hundreds of eyes followed him from all quarters. Like kicking up mosquitoes walking through a peat bog. Even the cockroaches seemed nervous.

Quack. Quack.

Honk. Honk.

A highly unusual situation.

'Professor, we have the technology nailed down, but you must continue to work with us – help us.' It was Gribuchevitz, Flaffanoff's boss.

'Work with that ignoramus poking his long nose into everything?' The professor pointed at Flaffanoff.

'He's not an ignoramus. His father fought alongside Vladimir Illych – was in the party – fought with Rykov.'

'With whom?'

'Rykov – it doesn't matter. He was erased from the history books.'

'And this new one, this queer bird with a long neck and no shoulders?' The professor pointed towards a new character who'd arrived on the scene that morning.

'That's Durfdovich. He's an associate.'

'Of what?'

'The Sadko and Vinzetti Institute for the study of dying capitalist institutions.'

'What's Sadko and Vinzetti? It sounds like a Hungarian wine.'

'They're foreign patriots. In Italy. Philadelphia, I think.'

'I don't like him,' the professor said, patting Ivanushka the goose on the head, pointing towards Durfdovich with his free hand. 'He stares too much. Look! He never blinks.'

'He doesn't miss a thing.'

'His eyes are too small, set too far apart. Shifty! He fidgets all the time.'

'What do you expect from an intellectual?'

The professor didn't seem convinced.

'We can't help how anyone looks, Professor,' Gribuchevitz said. 'You're no prize yourself, you know.'

The professor shrugged his shoulders. Ivanushka picked at some plump pumpkin seeds the professor held in his hand. 'And that one – the short man without a shadow?' asked the professor, pointing at a man about a metre tall.

'That's Bitonich. Miniaturization.'

'Miniaturization?' asked the professor. 'You need smaller geese?' Ivanushka cringed. The professor patted down his ruffled feathers.

'Your design, professor. Your methodology – whatever you call it.' Gribuchevitz impatiently cast his beady eyes around the laboratory. 'It will be of great application for the party. It works.'

'Then leave me alone! Go away!'

'Our work is not done.'

'How?'

'It is too big – the equipment. It must be made smaller. That's Bitonich's job. He makes things small.'

'He looks too small to do anything.'

Ten

'Kvak. Kvak.'

'Keep trying, Vasenka.'

'I can't do it, Arnold. You – you're so smart. How do you do it?'

'I don't know,' Arnold replied, wrinkling the edges of his

beak pensively. 'I just do it.'

'Honk,' said Ivanushka.

'Honk,' said Arnold.

'Why, you sound just like a goose! More like a goose than I!'

No one knew how Arnold came to be a bilingual duck. There were rumours of a mixed heritage, gossip about an errant ancestor from Kamchatka who flew over the straits, courted a Canadian duckette, then flew south with her for the winter.

'Qva-ack. Quack.'

'Much better, Vasenka. You'll do it yet!'

'You can do it, Vasenka! You're almost there!' Ivanushka added.

Vasenka waddled with pride, and the other Soviet ducks looked on with envy. 'We too will have a bilingual duck,' they said, shaking their beaks proudly as they followed after the American duck, the Soviet duck and the Ukrainian goose.

Eleven

Four months later, things had become smaller at the institute. Even the portrait of the institute's founder, Comrade Tikvin, seemed to shrink in size where it hung, over the crooked archway in the foyer. Still the same expression on his face. Apprehensive.

The professor had lost weight. He scowled all the time, shaking his head and wagging his finger at Bitonich, expert at miniaturization, wherever he could find him.

The geese and ducks got smaller too, the grain problem being what it was. Feed was hard to come by, the capitalists playing games with weather and the world market. Even state security had trouble getting feed for the Priority One mission at the institute. Vasenka looked lean, and his feathers lost their lustre. Arnold looked gaunt, almost like a Soviet duck. He'd lost the little rings of healthy flesh around his bill and webbed feet.

For the ducks and geese, things eventually got better. Men in black quilted work uniforms started delivering sacks of grain weekly. The cloth sacks had deceptive markings the KGB had nearly blocked out. Words like 'Grown in Kansas' or 'Product of Illinois'. It was a capitalist plot, sticking the names of dying capitalist empires on the sides of Soviet grain sacks. The ducks and geese survived the international crisis despite the foreign interventionists. Most regained the weight they'd lost.

Things in the institute got smaller in general, except for Lydia Ivanovna, who came in later and later every day, after breakfast in the public cafeteria on the corner of Bashmakovsky and Poprishchin. The manager proudly remarked that he had filled his yearly quota by March, thanks in large part to Lydia Ivanovna.

For lunch, she spread the morning edition of *Izvestiya* over her desk (over the ringing phones too), and chomped on three or four pirozhki (which had also got smaller, although their prices remained the same). Late in the afternoon, Lydia took a 'nourishment break', as she called it, and ate cold, starchy noodles from a net sack. Then she hurried home for supper. Lydia, in short, had not got smaller.

The things that were reduced the most were the professor's devices. When Flaffanoff had first arrived, the professor's laboratory had looked like the innards of a giant machine. It was impossible to tell where the device – the 'apparatus', as the professor called it – ended, and where the spare parts began. It was like walking around inside a giant clock that didn't work.

Bitonich and his team of lackeys and miniaturization specialists had done well. The apparatus got smaller and smaller. Chunks and pieces of the older, clunky versions stood stuffed in the trash bins in the institute's courtyard – rejected, like Lydia in love, for being too big.

Bitonich's first attempt at a miniaturized machine was about the size of a Moskvich sedan, and as ugly. Then came one about the size of a keg of kvass or beer. The next one looked like a television set without a screen.

A thin smile spread across Bitonich's small face the day he invited his superior in for a demonstration.

'Our miniaturization is completed,' he beamed. 'Our mission is fulfilled!' His tiny arm waved proudly towards the screenless television.

'You've only just begun, mouse!' the superior person barked. 'We'd need at least five collective-farm workers to haul that thing around!'

'You mean – you mean,' Bitonich's little voice trembled, 'You mean it has to be carried around?'

'Smaller than that, pipsqueak! It has to be invisible,' the important person said. 'Don't bother us again until you've finished!' he added, as he shuffled out the door, four gloomy (but small) assistants rushing out after him.

Bitonich went back to his little drawing-board, back to the tiny books in his library. He called in extras for the emergency mission. A peasant from Krasnoyarsk who'd made a watch so small you needed a forty-power microscope to tell what time it was (he'd been sent to Krasnoyarsk from Moscow for that one). An engineer from Vladivostok who made a car so small you needed tweezers to open the door.

'But it gets 1,287 miles to the gallon!' he protested as they pushed him out of his Leningrad research institute position into early retirement.

Six months after Bitonich's boss left in a huff, Bitonich

summoned him proudly back. The professor's apparatus had been reduced to the size of a ring.

'The ring's ugly!' Hlafdarvich the superior boss said, frowning like a schoolmistress, turning his nose up at Bitonich's masterpiece of miniaturization. 'The stone's too big – the setting's too bulky!'

Hlafdarvich himself was about four foot seven. He looked like the type of male who would worry about the looks of a ring. A tiny, pointed nose. A sharp, pointed chin. Little eyes, set closely together. He was a good size for his position in life, head of the Gorky Institute for Miniaturization and Small Things. You couldn't see his shoes under his trouser legs.

'The world will never be the same, comrades!' the little man without feet said the next time Bitonich beckoned him to the institute. 'Imagine! A machine that makes people say what they don't want to say!'

He rolled the tiny device across his palm. 'And the size of a ring!' He held it up to his little face, peering at it through his tiny round lenses. 'An ugly ring, however. Bitonich!'

Twelve

'It would be better if we didn't need the professor,' Hlafdarvich told Bitonich as they stood in the institute elevator. 'I don't understand why we need the old coot.'

The elevator jerked. There was a loud scraping sound, and the elevator came to a halt halfway between the second and third floors.

'Achoo!' Bitonich sneezed from the dust settling down the shaft from the spot where the elevator scraped the plaster wall. Hlafdarvich wiped his shoulder and cheek, then jabbed at the elevator buttons.

'To the devil with your sneezes!' Hlafdarvich bellowed. 'And to the devil with these foreign elevators! To the devil with the professor too!' he added. 'Why do we need him?'

'The apparatus works only when the professor activates it,' Bitonich said meekly, grabbing at the elevator bars.

'Why?' Hlafdarvich asked, jumping up and down, then stomping his feet. He was impatient. He didn't like things that couldn't be pinned on to a circuit board or wouldn't take bribes, at least. He didn't like his children. Misha wore foreign, decadent jeans, and Tanya brushed her hair all the time and chewed gum whenever she could beg any off a foreigner.

'Brainwaves. That's the secret,' Bitonich said, wiping his little head and peering upward, through the open grid of the elevator roof. Two duck bills peered back at him from the third-floor opening, and a white goose's neck bent gracefully, curiously downward.

'He won't tell us?' Hlafdarvich crawled through the little trap door at the top of the elevator. Bitonich followed.

'We could make him tell us,' Hlafdarvich said as he pulled his partner up by the arm.

'And ruin the project? Threaten the deadline? We meet the big leader, the premier, next week. We screw this up, and we'll both be shaping ice cubes in Kamchatka!'

The two little men inched up the elevator cable.

'Quack,' said Arnold.

'Kvak,' said Vasenka.

'Honk,' said Ivanushka, wrapping his neck into a knot and gnawing at the cable.

'I'll wring that damned goose's scrawny neck!' Hlafdarvich threatened as he reached the third-floor opening. 'You'd think those little beasts – those barnyard fowl – understood us, knew what we're doing.'

Ivanushka let out a long, low honk. He and his two duck

companions waddled down the hallway as Bitonich and Hlafdarvich crawled out of the elevator shaft.

Thirteen

'Come, Vasenka! Tell Arnold to hurry! We have some fresh grain in the lab for you fellows!' The professor walked up the steps towards the laboratory. Ivanushka pecked at the back of his knees.

'Look! The old coot is crazy! He talks to ducks,' Bitonich said, poking Hlafdarvich in the ribs.

'Shh!' Hlafdarvich whispered in reply. 'He'll hear you. Kamchatka! Remember Kamchatka!'

'To the devil with Kamchatka!'

'Ice cubes! Endless winter! No vodka! No women!' Hlafdarvich looked sideways at his partner. 'No boys either,' he added.

'Hmpff,' said Bitonich.

'Professor!' Hlafdarvich called out, motioning to Bitonich. 'Let's do the experiment again, like yesterday. With the ducks and the geese.'

'Again? We're tired.' The professor patted Vasenka, then Arnold on the head.

'Quack.'

'Kvak.'

'Once more, Professor, please!'

The professor took off his glasses, rubbed his forehead, and frowned. 'It's not working.'

'What's not working?' Hlafdarvich asked cleverly, winking at Bitonich.

'I can't activate it.'

'What activates it, Professor?' Hlafdarvich asked slyly.

The professor looked with contempt at the two little

intruders standing before him.

'You won't tell?' Hlafdarvich asked.

The professor shook his head. 'Brain waves, you roboticized morons, you bureaucrats! Brain waves!'

'What do you mean, brain waves?' Hlafdarvich asked, egging him on.

The professor looked impatient. 'Brain waves, you automaton! A certain thought pattern. You'd know little about that! A certain frequency. That's all.'

'Do it.' Hlafdarvich sounded like a boy giving out a challenge.

'I can't.' The professor too sounded like a boy.

'Try!'

The professor put on his spectacles, sat down at his desk. 'Will you leave us alone for the evening if we do it just once?'

'Yes,' Hlafdarvich replied, and Bitonich nodded.

The professor closed his eyes and rubbed the little ring on his finger. His hand snaked upward, his index finger making small circles in the air. It spun and spun, turned sideways, and stopped when it pointed towards the ducks and the goose.

'Honk!' said Vasenka.

'Kvak!' said the goose.

Hlafdarvich smiled, rubbing his little hands together. 'Now it's time to try it with people!'

'Tomorrow?' Bitonich asked. 'Randomly? In a crowd?'

'Yes, my little pipsqueak,' Hlafdarvich replied.

The professor opened his eyes and rubbed his forehead.

'Quack,' said Arnold.

'Honk,' said Ivanushka.

Fourteen

'Your lips smile, but your eyes are always sad.' Mary held Misha in the middle of the wide, sloping bed in a darkened corner of his Leningrad apartment.

'Were you always so sad?' she asked, brushing his lips lightly with her fingertips.

'It's not sadness.' He paused, and his eyes looked into hers. 'It's the way I am.'

'But your poems sing with life!'

'Maybe that's where it all goes,' he said, stroking her temple, then touching her lashes. 'And your eyes have a longing for sadness, I think.'

'For depth. They're looking for depth.'

She hadn't found it before. A young twenty-four-year-old. Georgetown University. A father who steered her towards law, an international career.

'Learn Russian, Mary,' he'd said when she turned seven. 'It will stand you in good stead.'

And when she turned ten, he said, 'Always have something other people demand. A combination of things others don't have.' He'd worked for the state department, died of a heart attack at forty-six, when she was a sophomore. Her mother had died in childbirth.

Mary learned Russian, got her degree in international studies, and worked for the state department. She met Misha at a reception for visiting staff. She met Russian poetry through him.

'I – I never knew words could do so much!' she confessed.

'So much what?'

'Say so much – with such feeling – that's what I didn't

know. Feelings.'

'Yes. Feelings.'

'But such deep feelings!' she said, leafing through a small blue book with tattered, brown pages, a collection of Mandelstam's poems. 'Such sadness! Such longing! Such an urge for life!'

'It's called "toska".'

'I thought that word meant anguish or pain.'

'That too. But it seeks and searches. It's a driving force too.'

She'd found her own toska through Misha, who awakened it in her, breathing life into the closed rooms inside her head. She loved him, cared for him, desired him, talked and listened, and told him everything. He read poems to her, and held her when she cried.

'All my life, I've worked with things,' she said, lying curled up next to him on the bed. 'Facts. Events. A word was like – like a nail. Or like a grid on a map. An agreed-upon commodity.'

'Words are gems, mined from the soul,' he said, and they went for a midnight walk along the Fontanka Canal. It was June, and the streets glowed faintly in an ethereal light.

Fifteen

At first, it was decided that neither Arnold nor Vasenka nor Ivanushka would accompany the professor on the first test, or to the West later, when the world would reel from the professor's discovery.

'It would never work,' said Barvingtov, the fat KGB boss. 'In the West, we must be in high places, the very highest.' He frowned so hard that his furrowed brows met in the middle and crossed.

'I want them to come with me,' the professor said firmly but softly.

'Ducks?' Barvingtov bellowed, pointing a thick finger towards Arnold and Vasenka. Their little eyes blinked, as they stood, unmoving.

'An ugly goose?' he bellowed louder, pointing at Ivanushka who was, in truth, not such a bad-looking goose.

Ivanushka waddled towards the bathroom, hopped on to the ridge of the toilet, and peered into the dirty mirror, bending his neck in all directions.

'Honk!' He hopped off the ridge, waddled back to Barvingtov, and pecked at the seat of his trousers.

'A goose!' Barvingtov yelled, shaking his head and shooing away Ivanushka. 'Goose shit! It will not be allowed!' Barvingtov proclaimed, smoothing down the back of his trousers.

The professor stood in the middle of his laboratory, Arnold under one arm, Vasenka under the other. Their bills nuzzled up in the folds of his frock.

'We need the animals,' the professor said. 'They are part of the process.'

'It will never work!' Barvingtov announced, waving his arms helplessly towards a cowering Flaffanoff. 'Two ducks! One goes "kvak, kvak", the other "quack, quack". It will never work! Why, look at the professor! It will be hard enough to get him into high places!'

Arnold and Vasenka stretched out their necks and snarled, then bent their heads to look at the professor. It was true. The professor was a queer-looking human specimen. A body so thin it seemed not to exist under his frock. Two spindly little lines running straight down from under his frock, tiny shoes at the end. A thin face. Pinched nose. Tiny metal-framed glasses that hung crooked off his nose. A shock of snow-white hair exploding off the top of his head.

'How would you get anyone like that into a press conference or a summit meeting?' Barvingtov asked with despair, pointing at the professor.

'I don't care about your plans. I don't trust your motives. I don't care if you use us or not!' the professor answered, patting Arnold's then Vasenka's head. 'You can all go to the devil for all I care! Leave me alone with my experiments, with my animal friends! To the devil with all of you!'

Things seemed at an impasse. The professor snarled at Barvingtov. Arnold and Vasenka lowered their heads, as if ready to pounce with more ferocity than the duck world has ever seen. Ivanushka stuck out his long goosy neck, ready to peck away on command.

Barvingtov took a deep breath, waving his hands helplessly in the air. 'You need the ducks?'

'Yes.'

'Two of them?'

'Yes. The transfer doesn't work without the ducks,' answered the professor. 'We need the goose too.'

'That ugly goose?'

Ivanushka lowered his head, and his neck shot out like a ramrod as he walked slowly and deliberately towards Barvingtov.

'It's OK, Ivanushka. These people know nothing of taste,' the professor said. Ivanushka backed off from his prey, but Barvingtov rubbed the seat of his pants anyway.

'There's no other way?' Barvingtov asked, pulling in his rump.

'No. For the brain waves to go from one person to another – for the system to work, I need both ducks, and the goose too. Just like you need agents and interpreters, but more so.'

'Hmmf,' said Barvingtov.

'Quack,' said Arnold, peering around the professor

towards Vasenka.

'Kvak,' said Vasenka, peering back.

'They don't like us. They don't want us to go,' Arnold whispered.

'I want to travel abroad. See a bit of the world in my short duck-life,' Vasenka added, woefully. 'We can't even migrate here. It's forbidden to fly long distances without clearance.'

'Shush, you two worry-warts!' the professor whispered. 'We'll go. We'll go.'

'Oh, we'll never go! We'll never do anything!' Ivanushka wailed in a whisper.

'Ivanushka, you always think the worst of things!' the professor admonished under his breath.

'I've got it!' Flaffanoff leaped into the centre of the room. 'Remote control! We'll wire the professor and the duck. Bitonich can do it, I'm sure.'

'Remote control won't work,' the professor insisted. Flaffanoff's smile disappeared. Barvingtov threw him a dirty look, and Flaffanoff's usual frown returned.

'We'll see how we do tomorrow,' Barvingtov said with resignation. 'The test tomorrow will tell. The random test. With people.'

Sixteen

'My dearest! My dove! My little treasure! I hardly see you any more. They keep me so busy at the institute.'

The professor took off his hat and gloves. His heavy wool coat slid off his arms, and Sonya, his daughter, caught it, putting it to rest on the hook by the door.

'The samovar is humming, Papa. We'll have fresh tea in a moment.' She led him towards the little round table standing in the centre of their small apartment off Kalinin Prospekt.

She brought him a glass of steaming tea and a plate with slices of rye bread and malina jam. 'You look so tired, Papa,' she said, stroking his cheek. 'You retired years ago, you know. You shouldn't work so hard.'

The professor slumped in his chair, his bony hand following his daughter's hand as it moved across his forehead. 'You'll play for me?'

She nodded.

'Your music relaxes me. It takes my mind off other things.'

'You don't like your work any more, Papa?'

'I love my work. It's the people who bother me. They want to put everything to use. Everything must be for a purpose, you know,' he said wryly.

After tea, Sonya played the cello for her father. Dvořák. By the second movement, the professor dozed in his chair, his head rising and falling with his breathing, nodding gently forward, then back.

Seventeen

The doorman, of course, had to be bribed. The People's Bliss Restaurant couldn't just let in everybody, and if a person got in – that is, if he just walked through the door like a know-it-all capitalist tourist – well, that wouldn't do. Waiting and anticipation increase appreciation. If that isn't in Lenin's collected works, it should be. Besides, if a person has to wait for all good things, and if he doesn't have to wait to get into the People's Bliss Restaurant – well, the mind can draw strange conclusions when left to its own devices.

The doorman, of course, was just doing his job. The restaurant was full. Customers shouted for service, banging spoons on the round wooden tables, while others waited passively, with blank expressions, looking like trespassers or saboteurs. The supplicants leaned in at the door, wailing and swaying, holding out cards proving they were important personages, deserving of passage. 'I am Rykov's granddaughter!' one toothless old lady in a red and black scarf yelled.

'Who in the devil's name is Rykov?' the doorman asked, not caring to find out the answer. Such chaos. Such disorder. More than the restaurant could bear. The poor, overworked door bent in at the middle, its panes of glass rattling threateningly. It was a pre-revolutionary door. Those built after 1917 could stand more yanking, pushing and jerking.

Behind the door, like Moses holding back the flood, stood the fat, bald doorman, sneering at the crowd and giving them the finger when they pushed too hard or shouted too loud. A scourge of pleading Muscovites, yelling and shaking as if their lives depended on a tin bowl with a dab of ice cream and a paper-thin wafer.

'The granddaughter of Rykov!' the old lady repeated.

'Who's Rykov?' The doorman's hoarse voice carried through the door.

'Rykov's a nobody!' a fat man yelled, waving a card in front of the window. 'He's been dematerialized from history. He didn't exist! Here, let me in! I'm Brezhnev's cousin!'

'And Brezhnev almost doesn't exist!' a fat man shouted.

'Here, I've worked with the KGB!' a skinny man yelled, waving a card in the doorman's face.

'Everyone's worked for them!' the doorman shouted through the door. He sat down on a three-legged stool, a weary expression on his face, and pulled out a romance,

Love among the Tractors.

Comrade Flaffanoff, special projects, state security, pushed through the crowd and flicked his lapel out almost as fast as the eye could register. The glint of that little red pin – it could move Soviet mountains. It did. The doorman threw down his book, opened the door, stepped back, bowed and held it. In walked Flaffanoff, followed by Bitonich, the professor, Fat Lydia Ivanovna, Arnold, Vasenka and Ivanushka with smoothed-down feathers picked free of bugs.

'The barnyard birds – there are regulations, comrade comrade,' the doorman said half-apologetically, half-fearfully. Lydia Ivanovna craned her head forward, licking her lips, her fingers reaching out towards the pantry.

'The regulations will have to be suspended, momentarily,' Flaffanoff said with confidence. The doorman stepped aside, his back pasted against the wall, as his hand unwillingly rose in salute.

'Quack,' said Arnold as he passed.

'Kvak,' said Vasenka.

'Honk,' said Ivanushka, pulling at the doorman's shoelace.

Slam. The doorman shut the door on the rest of the pleading multitudes.

Eighteen

'My child, what is wrong? You look so sad, as if the world had deserted you.' The professor held his glasses to his face as he looked into his daughter's eyes, his bony hand running along her smooth cheek.

'I'm all right, Papa.' She wrapped her hand around his wrist, and her eyes looked down towards the floor.

'Tell me, child, what is it?' asked the professor, placing his fingers under her chin and raising her head so their eyes met. 'Tell me, child.'

'It's a man.'

'Well, you're twenty-two, my dearest. Its time has come, I would say.' He patted her head and made her sit down on the sofa. 'He is cruel to you? That's why you cry at night?'

'Oh no, Papa! Not at all!' she said, apparently almost offended.

'Good! Your mother and I,' he sat down next to her, 'we were married twelve years. God rest her soul. We never had a cross word, never quarrelled.' He took her hand. 'You have quarrelled?'

'Oh no, Papa!' She started to cry.

'What is it then?'

'He is – he's a – a foreigner.'

'You don't understand one another? That's the problem?'

His question had its intended effect. She smiled through her tears. 'He speaks Russian.' She paused, brushing the hair back from her eyes. 'We have an understanding, deeper than Russian or English, deeper than language.'

'He's an Englishman, is he?'

'No. An American.'

'An American.' The professor repeated the word, mulling over it, as if its syllables would reveal some secret. 'An American.'

'Yes.'

'Hmmm. A good man?'

'Yes, Papa. The best.'

'Then go to him. Go with him.'

'But you, Papa.' Her eyes watered more, as she looked into her father's eyes.

'Why, you little dummy! You think your mamasha and I brought you into the world to have you become an old maid? Go with your man!'

'Who will take care of you, Papa?'

'I will take care of myself, of course. And my work takes care of me.' She frowned. 'My work keeps me busy,' he continued. 'It gives me energy, something to live for.'

She seemed pleased with his answer, stood up, hugged him and offered tea.

The old man's hand trembled as he lifted the tea glass to his lips. 'What about this American? How is he here?'

'He's an exchange student.' She sipped her tea, looked down sadly. 'His visa expires soon, very soon.'

'Oh.'

'You could help, Papa?' She looked animated, nervous, desperate. 'Your connections at work?'

'My dearest,' he said, peering deep into her eyes. 'The kind of people who work with me, who look over my shoulder night and day – it's best for them not to know.'

Nineteen

'Why have you brought me here? I hate ice cream. I hate crowds.' The professor held on to his glasses as Flaffanoff pushed him through the packed corridor of the People's Bliss Restaurant.

'This is the test. We will try your method on people. Here.'

'Why here?' the professor asked. Flaffanoff shoved him from behind, wedging his way forward through the crowd. Old ladies scowled, and men grumbled. A cockroach skittered across the corridor, diving in and out between boots and shoes. Ivanushka the goose bent low to the floor, in hot pursuit.

'A random sampling,' Flaffanoff said, one hand at the

back of the professor's head, the other pushing into his ribs. 'Anonymously performed. In a crowd. The superiors demand it. You have the ring?'

The professor nodded, his head cradled in Flaffanoff's hand.

'Good! Sit here!' They'd found a table near the centre of the big, brightly lit hall. Arnold and Vasenka scooted under the table. Ivanushka waddled off towards the kitchen, and Fat Lydia followed. They returned a few minutes later, Lydia smacking her lips over a chocolate ice-cream bar.

'Oh, ah, comrade waitress!' Flaffanoff waved his little finger in the air. It was like a twirling worm in search of an apple. 'Comrade waitress, we should like some dessert here.' He tapped his fingertips lightly on the table. 'Some ice cream here, comrade, possibly – '

'Go to the devil!' the waitress snorted as she passed by, not looking at Flaffanoff, or where she was going.

'Quack.' She nearly stepped on Arnold.

'This is not the Moscow Zoo, you know!' the waitress said, glaring at Flaffanoff. 'Not a barnyard! Get these dirty beasts out of my station!'

Flaffanoff flashed his pin.

'Your little red pin means nothing to me, short person!' the waitress replied, brushing her hair out of her eyes. She tried to tuck the loose strands of hair back under her paper kerchief while her other hand balanced a tray with tottering, empty ice-cream containers.

Flaffanoff flashed his pin again.

'Quit flapping your jacket like a one-winged crow! Such hooliganstvo! See these animals here?' She pointed at her customers, not at the ducks or the goose. 'All these people bleating and mooing for ice cream? They all have pins too. You can't get in without one!'

Flaffanoff pulled out a card from his wallet and held it

boldly up to her eyes. Big black letters. Thick. Solid-looking. 'KGB. (Formerly MGB, NKVD, Cheka). Committee for Governmental Security. Special Projects Section. Highest of Highest Priorities.' And underneath, in bold red letters, underlined twice, 'Too high to categorize.'

'Hmmf,' said the waitress.

'Kvak.' Vasenka hopped up on a stool.

'I would like some malina-berry topping on my ice cream,' Bitonich said politely.

'We're out of malina-berry topping. It's out of season.'

'This is the season,' the professor replied meekly, correcting the waitress.

'Tell that to the suppliers!'

'I'll take chocolate topping on mine,' Flaffanoff said with authority.

'We're out of chocolate,' the waitress said with more authority.

'Plain ice cream then,' Flaffanoff said with exasperation.

'We're out,' she said triumphantly, straightening her paper kerchief.

'Then why in the devil's name are you open?'

'It's in the plan. We're always open on Tuesdays!'

'Why are all these people here if you have nothing to serve?'

'You shouldn't complain! It's a privilege to get in. It's easier on the days we have nothing to serve. Look around you. These people on stools, at tables. They're not complaining and moaning.'

Flaffanoff shook his head in bewilderment. Ivanushka chased after another cockroach. A juicy one. Nice short legs.

'If you're out of ice cream,' Flaffanoff began, like a grand inquisitor, 'then what is in those dishes you're carrying?'

'The chef's private stock. That's his relatives over there.'

She pointed towards a table. A fat woman. Two fat children licking their fingers. Other customers looked on with envy.

'Bring us some of his private stock, then,' Flaffanoff said menacingly.

'We're out!' the waitress replied, more menacingly.

Durfella Davidovna, the waitress, stomped away from the table, leaned up against the counter near the pantry, and leafed through a beauty magazine.

'Professor.' Flaffanoff's head bent low over the table. 'Now's the time for the test. Try out the ring.'

'Why? On whom?'

'On her! On the waitress. If it works on her, it will work on anybody.'

Twenty

It was fall in Leningrad. The lindens along the embankment had turned bright yellow, then faded into brown. Leaves fell, and empty branches waved in the wind.

'Too bad we're from different countries,' Mary said, holding on to Misha's arm as leaves swirled around their feet. They were walking towards the Moika Canal. Misha was silent.

'I leave in two weeks,' Mary said.

'I know. I wish it weren't so.'

A gust of cool wind channelled down along the low, swaying buildings lining the narrow canal and its walkway. Mary pulled her scarf tighter around her neck. The wind tugged at Misha's open jacket collar.

She'd spent five months in Leningrad, whisking out of the Europeiskaya Hotel on Brodsky Street early each morning, and walking slowly back, late in the evening.

Work was hard.

It had been spring when she arrived. Mud puddles then lay across sidewalks, and thinning lines of snow clung to the shadowed sides of buildings. Since her arrival, she'd met writers and union officials, negotiating. Copyright laws had changed, and there was hope for new publishing agreements between the United States, her country, and the Soviet Union. That's what had brought her to Leningrad, a twenty-three-year-old lawyer, and that's what had brought her to Misha.

He'd attended the consulate's reception that first evening, in the ballroom of the Astoria Hotel. His sad, penetrating eyes had sought hers out, then danced when her eyes met his. Boyish, searching eyes. In a man over forty years old.

That first night they met, they walked around Saint Isaac's Cathedral, past Peter's Bronze Horseman, to the Neva River embankment.

'Peter's facing the West, reaching out for it,' Mary had remarked that first night.

'In Pushkin's poem, the statue came alive – prevented love,' Misha had replied forebodingly.

Misha and Mary made a silent pact then, never to talk about winter, never to mention parting. Neither had broken the pact, until now, a cold October evening.

'Too bad we're from different countries,' Mary repeated as brittle, brown leaves swirled along the Moika embankment.

'Too bad we're from different worlds,' Misha replied, digging his hands deeper into his pockets. 'I'll miss you.' He turned up his coat collar. 'No, that's not the word. I won't feel alive without you.'

'I don't want to leave you, Misha. Ever!'

They paused, facing one another. His hands came out of his pockets and rested on her shoulders. They kissed.

'Eto nado doma!' ('You should do that at home!') a passing babushka said kindly, in a careful sing-song voice as she passed.

Twenty-one

Bitonich cowered on his stool, his head barely reaching over the table. Flaffanoff waved his little-finger into the air. 'Comrade waitress!' he said politely.

'Go to the devil! I told you to leave me alone!' Durfella Davidovna replied.

Flaffanoff winced, then winked at the professor. 'Now, comrade. Now's the time for the test.'

The professor closed his eyes and turned the thick ring around on his finger.

'Quack,' said Vasenka.

'Kvak,' said Ivanushka the goose.

'Honk,' said Arnold.

'Now!' said Flaffanoff, gesturing towards the waitress.

The professor's head nodded, and he breathed through his nose, long and loud. His finger rose in the air, twirled in fast circles, and like a digit or a pointer, found out the husky waitress.

Her face screwed up, and she puckered her lips. 'Quack,' she said. Then her face relaxed, more than they had seen, and she swooned, three times. 'Comrade friends! You look so famished!' She patted Bitonich on his little bald head.

'Such cute ducks!' she exclaimed, leaning low over the table. Her breasts swung back and forth. Arnold and Vasenka cringed, ducking the giant pendulums swinging overhead.

'What a handsome goose!' Durfella said. Ivanushka

nodded, sticking his neck out proudly.

'I'd like my ice cream with malina berries,' said the professor.

'Why of course! We have some fresh malina berries in the back!' she replied, smiling so that all her aluminium fillings showed.

'I'll have chocolate topping on mine,' Flaffanoff said, marvelling at the waitress's transformation.

'Me too!' Bitonich's high-pitched voice rose over the table, and he set his little hands on his paper napkin.

'Berries – just berries – no ice cream for Arnold, Vasenka and Ivanushka,' the professor said, nodding towards his feathered companions.

'Of course! Of course!' Durfella nodded, waving her hands gleefully in the air. 'Ice cream would be bad for their little digestions. Is it OK for this little one?' she asked, patting the top of Bitonich's bald head.

'Yes. It's OK,' Bitonich said excitedly. 'Extra chocolate, please, comrade waitress.'

The thick-legged lady dashed towards the pantry, the paper kerchief on her head listing to starboard. 'My lord! My lord! All these hungry nice people! A little ice cream! A little sweetness into their lives! Why, I must hurry!'

She scurried into the kitchen. Half the customers dashed out of the restaurant, *en masse*.

'It's a capitalist plot of some kind!' a woman screamed, yanking at the arm of her daughter and lunging towards the door.

'It's "SovTravFilms"! They're making another damned travelogue for those capitalist tourists who steal all our circus tickets!' a short man said with authority, tugging at the young lady still sitting on her stool. 'Let's get out of here, woman! We never want to be on film! Loafing during working hours! They'll catch us yet, the devils!'

'It is the devil himself! He's casting a spell!' wailed an

old babushka, pushing her three chubby charges towards the exit.

Those who stayed feasted on the richest ice cream they'd ever tasted, piled higher than they'd ever seen in pewter bowls. Malina berries, chocolate topping, cherries even, challenged the Marxist law of gravity and rolled luxuriously along the stems of the bowls.

Flaffanoff smiled, savouring each morsel. Bitonich held on to the end of his spoon, digging it into the sweetness and steering it towards his little mouth. Arnold and Vasenka pecked at fresh malina berries. Ivanushka feasted on an impromptu confection of cockroaches and berries.

And all around them, Durfella the waitress hovered, wiping Bitonich's little chin, sticking a napkin into the professor's collar, patting the ducks and the goose. Flaffanoff spilled a gob of chocolate on to his skinny KGB tie, and Durfella came rushing back from the kitchen with a glass of water and a clean white rag. 'Goodness! Such a pretty tie! We must not spoil it!' she said, dabbing the tie daintily.

A collective-farm worker sitting behind Bitonich leaned forward, beaming towards his wife and daughter. 'Family, we must come to the capital more often! People here are so friendly, so nice!'

The Tikvin Research Institute weapon was ready.

'The world will never be the same!' Flaffanoff repeated as they stepped out on to Kalinin Prospekt.

'And now for the Kremlin!' added Bitonich. 'Then the world! The capitalist world!'

The two ducks nodded as they waited for the green light on Kalinin Prospekt.

Twenty-two

'Do you think love is impossible?' Sonya's expression said he shouldn't agree.

'It's not only not impossible, it's impossible to believe otherwise.' David's Russian was nearly perfect.

They walked along Sparrow Hills. The tall spire of Moscow University rose like a dark finger behind them. Below, Moscow spread itself out like a cat on a carpet. Clouds rolled in from the west, golden under the late-afternoon sun.

'You think our love is impossible, David?' She liked pronouncing his name. 'David', as he told her it was pronounced in America. A long, broad accented 'a'. He liked it when she pronounced it the Russian way. Short 'a', accent on the second syllable.

'Our love is – it just is,' said the American David. 'You've talked with your father, the professor?'

'Yes.'

'And?'

'And what?'

'He doesn't object?'

'To what? Being in love?' Her eyes smiled warmly, and the sun beamed through the gathering, darkening clouds.

'With an American – a David – a long broad "a" in his name.'

'He doesn't object.' She took his hand more tightly in hers.

An old Moscow babushka passed, wagging her bony finger. 'Holding hands! Like schoolchildren! A scandal! Eto nado doma!' ('You should do that at home!')

The woman shook her head reproachfully, in a way that

said she didn't mind.

'But David – your country. My country.' She took him by the arm. 'Would they allow it? Is it impossible – our love?'

'It is. It exists. They can't do anything about it.'

'But – but your visa's up in two months.'

'Marry me, Sonya. Get your father's blessing.'

'I have my father's blessing. He wants to meet you.'

'Marry me, Sonya.'

'Yes, David.'

They'd met in the spring. She was in the Academy of Music, playing the cello in the practice room on the first floor of the old stone mansion off Tolstoy Street.

He'd walked by. 'I heard heavenly music,' he told her later. 'I was drawn off the sidewalk, through the gate, into the building.'

'You could have been kicked out, you know.'

'I followed the strains of the heavenly music. The doorman smiled and nodded as I passed. I must have been under a spell too. Then there you were, all radiant and bright, like a vision. You in white. The brown cello.'

'Yes. I was playing Dvořák. I saw you out of the corner of my eyes. Blue eyes that sparkled cold, then warmed when I looked at you.'

'It was love at first sight, Sonya.'

'Yes, it was. Everything will work out, David?'

'It will. It will. I love you.'

'I love you.'

A spring breeze blew at fragile buds, and lilacs waved to one another.

Twenty-three

Pedestrians scattered like pigeons as the black Chaika limousine sped past the GUM department store, across the thick, grey bricks of Red Square, towards the Kremlin.

Ivanushka sat importantly in the rear seat, his neck bending in all directions (albeit with grace and dignity), to catch the passing panorama. Arnold and Vasenka stood on the small upholstered platform behind the rear window. Whenever the car hit a bump (which, given the realities of Soviet pavements, was often), the two ducks bounced on their little orange webbed feet, their feathers rustling slightly.

'Red Square!' Arnold said with awe. 'I thought the bricks would be red, but they're grey, just like all the bricks on the street in front of the institute.'

'You expected red bricks?' Vasenka asked.

'Well, in Kansas, we have the yellow brick road, or so I'm told, and it's actually yellow.'

'Must we go so fast?' the professor asked Flaffanoff.

'These people wouldn't know we're important, unless we went fast,' Flaffanoff replied. 'Comrade driver, hurry it up!'

The comrade driver lowered the kapochka on his head, put both hands on top of the wheel, and leaned forward so that his nose almost touched the windscreen. The car zipped past leaping pedestrians, on towards the open mouth at the base of the Ivan Bell Tower. The car spun hard to the right once inside the Kremlin.

'Our demonstration, comrade minister!' Barvingtov announced importantly when the great security comrade minister entered the reception room.

'Hurry it up. We're busy!' the minister said sourly.

The giant double doors squeaked open a second time, and in walked the great comrade premier himself, surrounded by bodyguards. The great comrade was not nearly as big as his portrait on the wall, but he held his shoulders high, as if he were. Each of his guards was a metre taller, but they stooped and cowered, as if to hide their comrade's shortness.

'Show me the plan provisions on this project!' The great one's voice bellowed from out of the circle of bodyguards.

'There are no plan provisions, your great shortness,' Barvingtov replied. His voice trembled.

'Show me the documents – the papers!' the voice of the short one commanded.

'There are none, comrade short one.'

'You're wasting my time! I'm too busy for nonsense. The Motherland waits! No plan? No documents? No provisions? Your scheme – it doesn't exist!'

Flaffanoff quivered. He opened his mouth. Nothing came out. Or, if it did, it was swallowed up in the great hall.

'Speak!' The great comrade stepped out of the circle of bodyguards and peered like a dentist into Flaffanoff's open mouth.

'Great comrade – your excellency – your superior personage – your high –'

'Get on with it, boy!'

'Great comrade – your excellency –' Flaffanoff stammered, his tongue getting caught in his mouth. He had never spoken to a great comrade before, not even to a minister or a deputy.

'Get on with it, twit!'

'This is – is a demonstration – proof of the possibilities – the ultimate weapon, your great smallness.'

'Shut up and get on with it!' the great voice boomed. The chandelier tinkled. The great comrade grabbed the minister by the ear. The minister winced and cowered. 'Comrade minister, if you're wasting my time, heads will roll! You'll find yourself running a day school in Novorossisk – tomorrow!'

'Get on with it!' the minister said in a squeaky voice, trying to imitate the great comrade.

'Get on with it!' Barvingtov barked at Flaffanoff in the same tone.

Flaffanoff turned to the professor, opened his mouth, and – and nothing came out. Flaffanoff tried snapping his fingers. That didn't work either. He almost went into a convulsion, but managed during all of his twitching and writhing to point to Ivanushka.

'Honk,' said Ivanushka.

'Kvak,' said Vasenka.

'What is this? A circus act? It's a piss-poor one, you dunderheads!' the great short one bellowed.

'Quack,' said Arnold.

'Quack? What is this foolishness – this aberration of the animal world?' the premier asked, tweaking his minister hard by the ear.

'Arnold's an American duck,' the professor said, bending down to pat Arnold, and glaring at the great one.

'Quack.'

'Kvack.'

'Honk.'

The animals rubbed beaks.

'What is this perversion?' the short one asked. 'Give your demonstration! Now! Or you'll all be in Kamchatka – by morning! What is all this foolishness?'

'T-t-t-transfer,' Barvingtov managed to blurt out.

'Thought transfer? We have that, dunderhead!'

'M-m-m-motive transfer, comrade sh-sh-shortness.'

'Do it!' Barvingtov commanded.

'Professor,' Flaffanoff said slowly, stammering. 'Do it.'

'On whom?' the professor asked calmly.

'On who you want – whom you want – on whoever!' the comrade premier waved his hands impatiently. 'On the minister!'

The minister leaned back on his heels. 'On me?' he asked in horror.

'On him!' the great comrade commanded, pointing his chubby finger at the minister.

The professor turned the ring around on his finger, rubbed it, closed his eyes and swayed on his feet. His finger raised in the air, a thing on its own, spun around like the needle on a crazy compass and stopped when it pointed at the minister.

'Quack,' said Ivanushka.

'Kvak,' said Arnold.

'Honk,' said Vasenka.

Twenty-four

Professor Tatiana Yanovska, Philology Department, Moscow University, was having problems with her American tutorial student. 'You must not analyse so much, David. Take things as they are. Accept them.'

The professor leaned back, her head nearly touching the row of books stacked on sagging shelves behind her high leather chair. 'Let things be what they are. You study them to death!'

'But the fantasy is so interesting.'

'Fantasy?'

'Yes – the fantastic. The imagined – the make-believe. Its construction intrigues me. I want to take it apart and look at it.'

'Then you should be a watch-maker, not a student of

literature. What do you mean by "fantastic"?'

'The contrived, the –'

'David.' The professor's voice was filled with admonition, pity too, almost. 'It is all true. It must be taken as true.'

'True? These stories – this fiction? A man who loses his nose? A ghost who steals overcoats?'

'He writes the truth – more so than other writers.'

'Gogol?'

'Yes, David. Gogol-Yanovski. His truths are greater perhaps than other truths. More easily grasped, too.'

'Yanovski? Is that his real name?'

'Yes.'

'Are you related, professor?'

'I don't know,' she replied with a twinkle in her eye.

'Where does the word "gogol" come from? I don't know what it means.'

'It's a type of wild duck, I think. Ukrainian.' Her eyes twinkled more. 'I want you, for our seminar, to put down your Tolstoy for now. Read Gogol. Only Gogol. One twentieth-century writer too.'

'Who, Professor Yanovska?'

'Bulgakov. *The Master and Margarita.*'

'I've read it. That's the phantasmagoric novel, right?'

'It's the truth, David. Consider it as truth.'

David looked puzzled. 'But phantasmagoria – everything's all mixed up. Jesus and Pontius Pilate. Woland – the devil in Moscow. Jerusalem. Matthew the Levite. It's crazy.'

'No, David.' Tatiana leafed through a book on her desk, patting its pages tenderly. 'Life is crazy. The book is the truth. When you come to see that life is crazy, then you will be sane. Complete, and whole.'

'But the purpose of literature is to show order – give meaning to life.'

'Put down your Tolstoy,' the professor said kindly. 'You need a massive dose of Gogol. Bulgakov too. That's your prescription. Now on with you! I have other students too, you know.'

When her student walked out of the room, Professor Yanovska picked up the telephone. 'There's hope, brother. There's hope.'

Twenty-five

The minister blanched as the professor's crooked digit pointed his way. Never in his life had he seen such disorder. Here in the great hall of the Kremlin, a scraggly professor in a dirty white frock – not even a party member. Two scruffy KGB lowlifes, the kind who chase after parasites selling black-market jeans. Two ducks rubbing beaks like animal perverts. A long-necked goose. And now the professor was facing him, rubbing his ring, and the minister felt tired, wanted to lie down and take a nap. No, fall asleep for a spell, standing up.

The room spun around. He didn't care. The great one, the short one, stared at him with malice. He didn't even care about that. The professor's finger pointing at him, and animal sounds filling the room. Duck sounds. One Russian, one suspiciously foreign-sounding. A kvak and a quack. Intermittent goose honks.

Then the minister's eyes blinked, and he became super-alert, pliant, wanting to talk, more than he'd ever wanted to do anything.

'Go ahead! Try it now, great comrade,' Barvingtov suggested to the premier, with a twinkle in his eye like that of a capitalist salesman.

'Try what, you Marxist nonentity?'

'Ask the minister something. Anything.'

'Hmfff, said his regal shortness, turning away from Barvingtov towards the minister. 'Comrade minister, how goes it with the plan in your ministry?'

'What plan? There's no plan. The place is a mess!'

The bodyguards fell back, as one body. The short one stood his ground, stepping forward, with interest. His nose almost touched the chin of the minister. 'Yes, comrade minister? Tell me about it.'

'Bribes all over the place! Chaos! Disorder! The cosmic abyss!'

'Tell me all, comrade minister!' the premier said, clasping his hands behind his back.

'Where could I start, comrade premier? Factories that don't exist. Except on paper. Workers – real workers, not paper workers – getting paid for working in factories that don't exist. Laziness and corruption like you've never seen!'

'Yes? Yes? Go on!' The premier was hungry for more.

'The economy's in a shambles! Selling fish of the "third freshness" – imagine! Our "second freshness" is spoiled. It stinks! Can you imagine what the third freshness is like? Phew!'

'Yes? Go on!'

'Coffee. We can't raise the price so we shrink the cans. Now they're so small, our Soviet can-openers can't open them.'

'Yes? Yes?'

'Our noodles! Our good old Russian noodles! They're all paste! They turn to soup!'

'And you, comrade minister? What about you, personally?'

The comrade minister burst into laughter, holding his hands on his stomach. 'Why, I've taken nine months' vacation this year! In Yalta! With my mistress! Six-day weekends in my dacha in Serebrenny Bory. Can you imagine? A six-day weekend! It's a Marxist contradiction in terms, it is! Hah! Hah! A Marxist contradition in terms!'

The minister bellowed, and the bodyguard cringed.

'Enough! Enough!' The great comrade stepped backwards, his mouth open, fingered the edge of his desk, coasted around to the far side and sat down in the great leather comrade-leader chair, rubbing his forehead. He turned towards Flaffanoff. 'This is – it's amazing! How do you do it! How do you get him to say such things?'

'Thought transfer,' Flaffanoff said boldly and proudly.

'Motive transfer.' The professor corrected him.

'What do you mean?' the great short one asked.

'Transmigration of motives. A biochemical chain reaction,' the professor explained. 'Through the material in this ring, a certain metal. Then through Arnold there, the tall thin duck. The oil in his feathers. Then Vasenka, the squat duck. His oil and subsonic vibrations. Then Ivanushka the goose. From him on to the target brain – here, in this case, your minister.'

'Amazing!' said the short one. 'How does it work – how does it make people say what they say – what they don't want to say, like my minister there, cowering in the corner. How?'

'The cerebral cortex,' the professor began. 'Vibrations caused by the presence of chemical vapours – it's quite complex, but quite easy too, once you understand the process. You see, the – '

'I don't care about that scientific stuff!' said the short one from behind his tall desk. 'Will it work on anyone?'

'Yes. On anyone.'

The great one beamed.

'A powerful weapon!' said Barvingtov, lighting the short one's stubby cigar.

'Honk,' said Ivanushka.

'What a weapon!' A cloud of smoke billowed above the comrade leader. 'We'll do it! In Washington. This month!' The great one's voice filled with joyful anticipation. 'The peace conference!' he licked his chops and puffed on his cigar. 'Can you men be ready?'

Barvingtov looked at Flaffanoff, who looked at the professor, who looked at Vasenka. Arnold nuzzled up to Ivanushka.

'Yes,' said the professor.
'Yes,' said Flaffanoff.
'Yes,' said Barvingtov.
'Honk,' said Ivanushka.

'Remember! Heads will roll if it doesn't work! Siberia for all of you!'

Vasenka and Ivanushka shivered.

Twenty-six

A heavy fog rolled into Leningrad in the morning, and by afternoon a misty drizzle filled the air. The buildings stood impatiently along the embankments, like so many sweating old ladies, huffing and puffing white steam.

'Soon it will be winter,' Misha said as he and Mary walked up Nevsky Prospekt.

'The city's so beautiful in the fog,' Mary said. 'Look! There's a line of light cutting through the fog. It's beautiful! Other-worldly!'

'Peter is other-worldly.'

'Peter, the person?'

'No, Mary. Peter, the city. Sometimes we call our city simply "Peter". It's a city not of this world, but another.'

Dark, fine hairs curled on Mary's damp forehead. Misha pulled up her rain-hood and tied a bow in the drawstring under her chin. 'Here, my dove, let's walk under the columns. It's dry there.'

They had walked up to the Gostinny Dvor building, girded by its yellow stone arches.

'Imagine the wind howling down through this portico on a frosty winter night,' Misha said.

Mary shivered. 'I can imagine it.'

'Imagine, then, a poor government clerk, bundled up in his new overcoat. His coat's stolen – right about here. The only thing he treasured in life.'

'How sad!'

'He dies. His ghost comes back, searching for his overcoat.'

'Akaky Akakievich?'

'Yes. Gogol. This is Gogol's city.'

'Such fantasy stories!'

'Not fantasy, Mary. It's the truth. Maybe truer than anything else you'll read about this city.'

'Ghosts and devils and a man losing his nose?'

'True. All of it true.'

'What do you mean, true?'

'True. Just what it says.'

'Fiction-true?'

'No. Life-true. Like mythology.'

'Well, I know that's true in a larger sense. Even though in a smaller sense, none of it is true.'

'Then think only of the larger sense. The smaller sense is a waste of time.'

They walked up Nevsky, caught a streetcar on Liteiny that glided along its iron rails towards his apartment. Sparks flew from the line overhead, and the trolley lights winked as they bumped over tracks criss-crossing the intersections.

'You know,' Misha began, brushing small raindrops off Mary's cheeks. 'In Greek, there are no separate words for "fiction" and "non-fiction". All of it is true.'

'In Leningrad, in this unworldly place, yes, for sure. Everything is true.'

'Other places too. We're going to Moscow next week?'

'Yes, Misha. I'll meet your mother?'

'Yes.'

'What does she do?'

'She reads poetry. To herself now. When I was young, she read it to me.'

'But what does she do to support herself – for a job?'

'She works in a research institute. But she sneaks a look at her books every chance she gets.'

'I look forward to meeting her.'

They'd ridden beyond their stop. They left the trolley three stops past his apartment. The streetcar continued on, forlornly, single-mindedly.

'People are like that,' Misha said, pointing down the avenue towards the trolley. 'They get on a track, grind on ahead, resolutely.'

'I was like that too, Misha.'

'I know.'

They walked back to his apartment. Misha made tea and laid their wet clothes carefully over the radiator. They made love, while raindrops formed and fell on the windowpane.

Twenty-seven

'I don't know what it is,' the great premier told Anniutochka his wife as he turned off the bedroom light and pulled off his trousers.

'How can you rely on it if you don't know what this thing is?' she asked, putting down her romance novel. It was the high point of the story. Ivan had met Katya. They'd fallen in love and deviated from their work schedules. They had just seen the light, rejoined the construction collective, and over-fulfilled their brick-laying quotas.

'It works,' said the great premier, pulling off his T-shirt. 'The professor explained it.' The premier's arms got caught in the T-shirt. 'Transmogrificationism or something. Biomedical activation.' He huffed and puffed as he struggled to work his arms free. 'Motivation – transfer of motivation. I don't understand it, but it works.'

'Be careful, Tolechka! It sounds like the work of the devil to me. A spell from Beelzebub himself!'

'We're atheists, you know!' the premier announced triumphantly, freeing his arms from their cotton entrapment. 'We don't believe in any of that supernatural stuff any more.'

'Not in God, maybe. But the devil, yes. Still the devil.'

'You're talking nonsense, Anniutochka. Non-Marxist nonsense. Antiquated thought patterns. Bourgeois inventions.'

'I'm talking the devil, Kolechka! He's not a bourgeois invention!'

'There is no such thing, woman!' The great leader stepped out of his trousers.

The old woman took out her teeth, laid them on the bedside table. 'Mog! Mog! Bekel and Begog!' she said, chanting.

'That's nonsense you're saying, Anniutochka!'

'That's Ezekiel! Verse thirty-nine. Don't blaspheme in this house, Kolya!'

'Anyway. It's science. Marxist! Soviet biomedicine! Not a spell or the devil.' The great one took off his elevator shoes and lost several centimetres in stature. He put on his flannel pyjamas, fidgeting with the fly. 'Damn buttons!'

She buttoned his fly for him, patting the great one's

small butt in the process. 'It all sounds like the devil to me, Kolechka.'

'It works. Why, they had a waitress falling all over herself, serving her customers.'

'Where, in Moscow?' she asked sceptically.

'Yes. Right here in Moscow! Can you imagine?' The small one grinned from ear to ear.

'Now it really sounds like the devil!'

'You haven't heard anything yet! I had the minister of the interior –'

'That lying, scheming pervert?'

'Yes, that lying, scheming pervert – he told me everything!'

'Then it's either the devil or a miracle!'

'I believe in neither,' said the great one, tucking the covers up under his chin. 'It's science. Another advancement of our great social science.'

Twenty-eight

It was late in the evening, and most of the lights in Moscow University had gone out. The city's most intellectual building stood like a giant black wedding-cake against a starry, dark blue sky.

'You've finished *The Master and Margarita*?' Professor Yanovska asked her American exchange student.

'Yes. I finished it,' David replied. The light from his professor's tiny goose-neck lamp illuminated a small oval on her desk top, and nothing else. 'I got completely caught up in the story. I couldn't put the book down,' he said, searching the darkness for the source of the voice asking the question.

'Good! There's hope for you yet!'

'But – but I don't believe in the devil,' he said shyly.

'Does the devil believe in you? That's the better question!' She turned the goose-neck lamp outward, illuminating her face, and she picked up a thick volume with 'Goethe' written in German script on the binding.

'It's all so – so insane. Crazy,' he said as she rubbed her palm across the book's cover.

'Life's crazy, David – the best parts of life.' She put down Goethe and leafed through the copy of *The Master and Margarita* on her desk under the goose-necked lamp's oval. 'The love story. The master. His Margarita.'

She looked up at him. 'Do you believe in love, David?'

'Yes, now,' he replied, thinking of Sonya.

'Good! There is hope for you. And Sonya? Does she love you back?'

David gasped 'Sonya? How do you know about her? Are you a clairvoyant or something?'

'Those terms are old-fashioned. But, no, I am not a witch, in the proper sense of the word.'

He leaned back in his chair.

'I am not a KGB agent either,' she added. The faint light from the lamp picked up the sparkle in her eyes.

'I never thought you were, professor.'

'I know Sonya, you see,' she began. 'Her father, the professor. He's my brother.'

'Oh, I didn't know – I want to meet him – Sonya said I will meet him.'

'When you are ready, you will.'

'When will I be ready? How do I "get ready"?'

'When you know that Gogol is true. You believe in love, David?' She repeated her question.

'Yes.'

'Love is crazy,' she said, her eyes looking deeply, unblinking, into his. 'It's illogical. Irrational. It can't be analysed or controlled or steered or started or stopped, you know.'

'I know.'

'Then you're almost ready. Soon you will meet the professor.'

Twenty-nine

Sonya and David sat on the sofa in the professor's living-room. A tall lamp with a yellow silk shade cast a warm glow about the room. The professor sat in his favourite armchair. His sister, Tatiana Yanovska, sat on a rocker to his left. Arnold and Vasenka frolicked underfoot, pecking away at the pattern on the red oriental carpet. Ivanushka was busy in the kitchen, honking at the back door while an alley cat teased him from the hallway. Its black paw swept back and forth in the space between the door and the floor.

'My sister and I have much in common,' the professor said, sipping his tea.

'Your last names are different,' David remarked, with a question mark in his voice.

'A scientist with a name like Yanovski – could you imagine it? And I work with ducks! How many jokes would that prompt, I wonder!'

'What's the connection with ducks? I don't understand,' David asked.

'Yanovska – Yanovski, that is – it's Gogol's last name,' Sonya said kindly.

'I know, but what's the connection with ducks?'

'Gogol – it's a Ukrainian word for a wild duck,' Sonya answered.

'Kvak, Kvak,' said Vasenka proudly, rubbing his bill along David's hand.

'So where does the name Proplavsky come from?' asked David.

'From *The Master and Margarita*, where else? Proplavsky was the ringleader for the magic show that took in all of Moscow, blurring the lines between fantasy, whatever that is, and reality, whatever that is.'

David smiled.

'Proplavsky lost his head,' the professor added. 'I should lose mine sometimes too!'

'Papa doesn't like contemporary, one-dimensional thinking,' Sonya said proudly.

'You mean, post-revolutionary thinking?' David asked.

'The revolution isn't the cause of it,' the professor replied. Professor Yanovska nodded in her rocker, letting her hand fall gently downward. Arnold pecked playfully at the palm of her hand.

'It's the twentieth century, David. That's the cause of one-dimensional thinking,' Professor Yanovska replied. 'The culmination of everything since Aristotle, Thomas Aquinas, Voltaire. Through the revolution. Movement forward – that's what everyone's been after. At the expense of the periphery.'

'Take me,' said the professor, nodding in agreement with his sister. 'I'm a scientist. I have two jobs then. To demystify things that are explainable, and to explain the unexplainable. Confound it – what a bore! It's like telling children over and over there's no Grandfather Frost, no Baba Yaga. No witches. No spirits.'

'And your second purpose?' David asked.

'More horrible than the first!' The professor's voice creaked, and his fingers shook with agitation. 'To take apart mysteries. And from the pieces, to make something practical. That's what's going on in my institute now. I have a miracle in my hands – a genuine wonder. Yet, these people who found out about it – they're dead set on harnessing it. They're the rapists of the human spirit, of the magic of life! Take! Take! Take! Destroy! That's what they want!'

'And that's what you do in your study of literature, David,' Tatiana added. 'You demystify. You try to disassemble things, explain them away.'

'That's what I did, professor,' David said, correcting her. 'Now, it's otherwise.'

'Yes! Good!' said Sonya. 'Find the mystery. Marvel in it. Share it. Pass it on. That's why I play the cello.'

'And you two are in love,' the professor said, not asking, looking first at Sonya, then at David.

'Yes,' said David.

'Yes,' said Sonya.

'Then marvel in your own mysteries! All four of them. You, Sonya. You, David. David's love. Sonya's love. Don't destroy any of them!' said the professor.

'How?' asked David.

'By just letting them be.'

Arnold and Vasenka quacked in agreement, and a long, gentle honk wafted in from the kitchen.

Thirty

Amerika. Vashinkton. The country has strange names. Wide streets choked with behemoth cars, probably brought in from the provinces to impress foreigners. Shag carpeting on everything. Artificial grass that never needs mowing. Store windows crammed with goods no plan could ever produce. Cabbages bigger than life – probably plastic. Monuments to the capitalists all over the place. Abraham Lincoln looks like a ghost, his knuckles as big as Amerikan cabbages. George Washington. It's good his monument is an obelisk, not a statue. On the Amerikan dollar, his face looks pasty and puffy, like a little girl puckering her lips. Undoubtedly a wig he's wearing too. So the dollar isn't such a beautiful thing. All dollar bills are one colour, whether they're one or one thousand. An Amerikan has to stay sober, stare at the pictures or numbers to know who's who, what's what. Amerika. You could never explain it to a Soviet citizen who's used to order and organization.

Everybody smells like a strawberry. They take two showers a week sometimes, maybe more. And in the pharmacies you find sprays for more parts of your body than you imagined existed, or smelled. Spray cans and roll-ons for armpits, crotches (male and female), shag carpeting, feet (male and female).

What's left, to smell like it should? Nothing. For places, they have aerosol sprays that smell like somewhere else. Pine-forest smells come out of the toilet, and the kitchen-sink drain smells like a mountain fireplace. No wonder Amerikans are so confused! Their smells makes them think they're somewhere else, wherever they are. No wonder the capitalist world is such a jumble!

Vashinkton's a showplace, a stage set. Laid out to trick gullible, gawking foreigners from the socialist, brotherly countries. Lord, how the countryside must suffer from what the leaders steal to make their capital look good!

Here and there are signs of weakness, cracks in their backdrop. There aren't enough banners and political posters in the capital. There must be a shortage of paper, or canvas, or imagination maybe. Can't these Amerikans think up enough slogans? 'Long live the decisions of the 86th congress!' 'Calvin Coolidge Lives!' Things like that should hang across Pennsylvania Avenue. It would add a sense of purpose. Workers united behind their Comrade President – that would make a political painting! It could cover a whole side of the White House.

On the first day in Vashinkton, the KGB decided that Flaffanoff looked too much like a Soviet citizen. Pedestrians stopped and stared at his lapels. Jealous probably. His were four times wider than theirs. Children poked fun at his tie. What do Amerikan children have against powerful stripes and bold polka-dots on durable, manmade Soviet material?

So the KGB agents pushed Flaffanoff into a tailor's shop on a crooked street not far from the White House. The old coot working there fretted over the Russian lapels, flapping them back and forth, shaking his head at the bold turn of the cloth, sighing, 'Khow sadd! Vat a vaste of klot!'

Twenty minutes later, Flaffanoff stepped back out from the dressing-room. He looked ridiculous. His suit was much too tight around the belly he pushed around when he walked. It (the suit coat, not the belly) had two slits at the rear, one on each side. Flaffanoff's wide bottom made the back of the coat look like half the roof of an outhouse.

The tailor span Flaffanoff around in front of a three-way mirror, shaking his head in admiration. Flaffanoff's face turned red from the tight, stiff shirt collar, but Durfdovich, the KGB interpreter, was pleased. So was the tailor, as he held his greedy hand out for his money.

'Tank you so much, comrade tailor!' Durfdovich said. He'd been in Amerika two months. 'I know what everybody should look like,' he said. But when he walked down the street, people's heads turned at his jeans and high-heeled boots with pointed toes. Children pointed at his skinny tie too.

The professor. The poor professor. He looked hopelessly out of place on Vashinkton streets. Even the tailor couldn't help. The professor looked like a piece of driftwood lost in the sea of a grey-wool suit that itched as he walked.

The professor. Durfdovich introduced him to the

gullible Amerikans as Dmitry Dobrovich, Associate Professor, Institute for the Study of Dying Capitalist Institutions. The Amerikans should have been honoured we had a whole institute for them. Instead, they took offence.

Durfdovich introduced Flaffanoff as the professor's assistant. Or so it seemed. No one knew what was going on, since everybody talked in English. People swallowed their sounds, said 'arrrr' a lot without trilling the 'r', and hardly opened their mouths except to smile, which was often, too often.

Arnold explained all this to Vasenka as they waddled around the city in the shadow of the professor, Flaffanoff and Durfdovich. There must have been a command from the CIA for all Amerikans in Vashinkton to smile whenever they spotted a foreigner, Vasenka decided.

The professor – Dobrovich, as he was called – was interested in agricultural questions and exchanges, Durfdovich explained. That accounted for the two ducks and the goose that accompanied him wherever he went. The dumb, smiling Amerikans took the bait.

Vasenka was intrigued with the way birds chirped, loudly, at will. He was saddened at the dearth of bugs in the capital. Too many sprays. And little yellow strips hanging in the supermarkets. In backyards at night, little contraptions with blue lights that went 'Zap!' whenever a bug flew nearby.

Arnold, as Vasenka's Amerikan host, wanted everything to be perfect for him. Ivanushka was likewise intrigued. He strolled around the Vashinkton gardens, following the professor's flapping grey trouser legs. No other geese in sight. 'Not one pretty little feminine goosechka in all the Amerikan capital?' he asked sadly. 'Just – just a lot of dirty pigeons?'

'All is not well in capitalism-land!' Vasenka told him.

Not everything was perfect in Capitalist-land, by any

means. Too many cars – all of them too big – so no one goes anywhere very fast. 'Beer too cold to drink!' Flaffanoff exclaimed.

'Vodka too warm to drink!' Durfdovich reminded him, shaking his long pointed head knowingly.

People rushed around all over the place. Horns honked. Cab drivers, possessed by evil spirits, stuck their heads out of taxis, shouting what could only be English profanities, 'Gett movink, ass-kholez!' waving their hands in the air. Super-expressway highways all over the place. Underground. Over the ground. Dogs on leashes, their owners scooping up their droppings in little silver shovels with long handles. Stupid-looking poodles wearing sweaters. Cats on leashes. A crazy place, with people walking around smiling all the time, clearly under a spell.

In short, the devil himself lived there, for sure.

Thirty-one

'You can't bring those barnyard ducks in here!' The square-shouldered, blue-uniformed Amerikan guard glowered with a toothy Amerikan grimace.

'I'm not bringing them in,' the professor answered calmly. 'They're coming in on their own.'

The guard didn't catch the logic. 'They're not allowed!' he thundered, waving his bayonet at the ducks.

'Come, Arnold and Vasenka. Let us go away from here – away from places where we're not welcome.' The professor turned about-face abruptly. Arnold and Vasenka did likewise, in unison.

'Vate! Vate djust a minoot!' Durfdovich the interpreter commanded. 'Dey haff to bee khere. Ducks – dey are needed,' he said. 'Goosenka too,' he added, pointing towards Ivanushka.

'Animals are not allowed in the Senate building!' the soldier boomed, his hat tilting forward.

'Dis is da land of da free?'

'Not for animals!' The soldier's hat bounced as he yelled.

'Dey haff visas and passport – deese animals!'

'I don't give a holy shit!' The soldier shook his head so hard his hat flew on to the floor.

'Ouch! What the –' Ivanushka had nipped the guard's finger.

'Goddam commie weirdos!' the guard yelled, sucking on his finger.

Thirty-two

The meeting of the peace council was not going well. Sounds of shouting filled the halls of the Amerikan Senate building.

'We want peace more than you do!' Durfdovich repeated what the Soviet ambassador had shouted, Durfdovich himself shouting as loudly.

'We want peace more than anything!' the Amerikan secretary shouted back. Durfdovich, the harassed interpreter, shouted louder. His face was turning red.

'We want it more than that, you slime!' the ambassador yelled.

'You've done everything contrary to peace for sixty years, you sons of bitches!' The secretary jumped up from his chair as he spoke.

The ambassador leaped to his feet as well. 'Tell me what he just said!' he commanded Durfdovich.

'You – you have not always – how to say it – supported

peace proposals.'

'And what else did he say, you snivelling coward?'

'He said – he said –' Durfdovich fingered the end of his skinny tie.

The ambassador grabbed it out of Durfdovich's hand and yanked him forward. 'Tell me exactly what he said!'

'He said – he said – he suggested – we have canine ancestors.'

The ambassador let go of the tie, and Durfdovich slumped to the ground.

'And you are imperialist bastards of the first order!' he shouted at the Amerikan secretary. 'Durfdovich, you tell them that – exactly!'

'You – you Amerikans – you engage in imperialist policies – you – your parents are not always married before they are born – before you are born, I mean.'

Two angry faces nearly met at the centre of the peace table. Poor Durfdovich's face was stuck in the middle. He put his hands up to his face and bit his lip as he translated.

Pandemonium broke out. The ambassador whacked the secretary on the head with a disarmament brochure. The secretary slapped the ambassador across the head with a treaty. 'Commie bastard!'

'Capitalist asshole!'

Durfdovich, fearing for his life and knowing something about the history of Hermes, refused to translate. Both the ambassador and the secretary knocked him to the floor and pummelled him.

The first meeting of the East–West Peace Council was not going well. Soon, functionaries and bureaucrats were punching one another, calling each other names. Papers flew, and tables came crashing down.

Flaffanoff came diving out of the tangle of squirming, pinching and biting bodies on the carpet. 'Professor! Professor! The ring! It's time for the ring! Please!'

Thirty-three

It was indeed time for the ring. Time to try anything. The capitalists were winning. The Soviet ambassador was holding his nose, yelling 'Ai! Ai! Ai! Ai!' The Amerikan secretary had landed him a good one with a left uppercut. Durfdovich translated each 'Ai!' faithfully, a loyal servant and party member to the end. To the end for him at that particular moment meant a kick in the groin from a capitalist attorney. Poor Durfdovich kept on translating, his voice getting higher and higher. He was bent over in agony, holding himself in ways best not expressed, howling like a spayed cat and jumping around like one too. It was not a pretty sight. Nor a particularly dignified one. The peace council was not going well.

'The ring! The ring!' Flaffanoff repeated, now down on the floor with a size 11½ Amerikan wing-tip at his neck. 'The ring, professor! For God's sake, the ring!' he gasped, tugging at the shoe.

The professor, who had miraculously remained outside the fray, leaned back in the fancy chair against the wall by the window, closed his eyes and rubbed the ring, holding his finger forward.

'Look!! That old commie coot's giving us the finger!' a fat senator shouted, lunging towards the poor professor. 'Get him! Get him!'

But before the senator, or anyone else, could reach him, the scene had dramatically changed, as it does when two dogs are gnawing and tearing away at one another, and someone throws five kilos of flour all over the place. It was that dramatic.

Everyone froze where they were, as if it all were a movie,

as if the 'Zenit 250' movie projector had gone on the blink, as they usually do.

'Kvak!' said Vasenka.

'Kvak?' asked a dumb Amerikan, imitating poor Vasenka. 'Even their ducks can't quack properly!'

'Quack,' said Arnold.

'That's better!' said the Amerikan.

'Quack,' said the Soviet ambassador, his head twitching.

'Kvak,' said the Amerikan senator, his face screwing upwards.

'Honk,' said the Amerikan secretary.

As if at a signal, people started getting up from the floor. Cameramen dusted off one another. 'Here, comrade Soviet photographer, let me dust off your lapel. My, what nice fabric!'

'Why thank you, comrade Amerikan capitalist. Your tie knot's crooked. Here! My, what a pleasant design! Such pretty colours!'

And so it went, people dusting off one another and straightening their jackets, as if they were all delegates to a polite people's convention and an elevator had just jostled them on the way to a smile seminar.

'It's quite hot in this room, my kind comrade,' the secretary said.

'Indeed, my Western friend. Indeed! Warm for us all,' said the ambassador.

Durfdovich took great pains to translate every polite word, smiling all the while.

'You like fishing, Mister Soviet Ambassador?' asked the secretary.

'Why yes, my good comrade!' answered the ambassador. 'I love fishing!'

'Well, good buddy, I know just the fishing-hole! Come on! Let's go!'

The Amerikan secretary and the Soviet ambassador

walked out of the room, arm in arm.

'Do you prefer minnows or grubs, pal?' the secretary asked.

'Grubs, my handsome companion,' the ambassador replied.

Durfdovich followed them out of the room. American and Russian newsmen, shaking hands, parted and let them pass, like the Red Sea before Moses.

'Let's all go downstairs for chocolate-chip cookies and ice cream!' a jolly journalist suggested, and the crowd filed out of the room, one by one, politely.

'After you, comrade!'

'No, no. After you, friend!'

Flaffanoff jumped up and down with glee in the nearly empty room. 'It worked! It worked! I've never seen anything like it!'

'The world will never, never be the same,' said the professor solemnly.

'Quack,' said Arnold, in agreement.

'Kvak,' said Vasenka, agreeing with Arnold.

'Honk,' said Ivanushka, agreeing with everybody.

Thirty-four

The Evanrood boat motor made funny noises, like a walrus gargling, as the plastic capitalist boat skimmed across a lake somewhere in Mariland, Amerika. The Soviet ambassador sat at the stern, holding on to his hat, bouncing when the boat cut through a wave. He looked covetously at the boat's padded red front seat, set high over the bow. It had a matching padded seat-back and a little spring that let you lean back now and then. The Amerikan secretary, sensing the gleam in the ambassador's eye, let him sit in the coveted seat.

The ambassador leaned back, testing the spring, and wiggled his butt on the thick capitalist cushion. 'Thank you for the honour – for giving me this wonderful seat, kind mister comrade secretary!'

'You can call me Bob. Bob Bunnybear's my name,' the secretary said, smiling. Durfdovich translated it all, mumbling as he tried to stick a worm on to his hook as the boat lurched across the water.

The secretary sat next to the Evanrood. He patted it kindly, like a pet dog. 'Don't push her so hard, Roger,' he told the CIA chauffeur who sat at the wheel.

When they anchored, the CIA man talked into a radio, and a small Coast Guard boat came out of nowhere and chased the other fishermen away. The secretary swatted the water the whole time with a thing he called a fly rod, not catching anything except a crick in his left arm.

The ambassador swung back and forth on his swivel seat high over the water, like a padishah, his bobber bouncing up and down in the water. 'The devil's mother!' he exclaimed as his fishing-pole bent downward. His round face rolled with sweat as he yanked the pole this way and that. His look of joy turned to one of sourness only a diplomat can have, as the slimy black head of a log surfaced at the end of his line.

'Wah!' the ambassador sobbed when his pole snapped in two. 'Chto za besobrazie!' he yelled as he tumbled into the water, head first. 'The devil! The devil!' he repeated while the secretary fished him out of the water, trying to pull him in by his feet (they were wrapped around the Evanrood).

Durfdovich caught four bass and a 'dogfish', as it was called. It looked more like an eel than a dog. Those crazy Amerikans can't see straight because smiling scrunches up their eyes.

Thirty-five

The professor chose not to fish. He, Vasenka, Arnold and Ivanushka walked along the shore. It looked like a procession. First a goose. Then a professor. Then two ducks taking up the rear, side by side. Sometimes the foursome stopped, gathering around in a circle, picking away at things in the sand.

'That man is a strange cookie,' the Amerikan secretary said, gesturing with his head towards the professor on the shoreline. 'Look at the way he nods his head. You'd think he was talking with them ducks or something!'

Thirty-six

That week, the capitalist newspapers carried headlines like 'Peace Talks Progress', 'Accords to be Reached', and 'President to Visit Moscow!'

The visiting Soviets were treated like royalty. At the receptions, Durfdovich stuffed himself, translating with his mouth full.

'Show some manners!' the ambassador commanded, chewing on a leg of lamb.

Durfdovich swallowed hard and blushed. A pickled herring slipped out of his mouth.

A picture of Arnold and Vasenka digging away at bugs appeared on the front page of the *Vashinkton Post* newspaper. Underneath was printed the caption, 'Accord between Russian and American ducks promises good things for people too'.

Crowds lined the capitalist sidewalks as the Russian delegation drove to the airport, and people cheered when they entered the plane.

The Amerikan secretary shook the ambassador's hand. The ambassador grabbed the secretary, planted a big smack square on his lips and one on each cheek.

Then it was Durfdovich's turn. As the crowd waved and the cameras rolled, he turned around on the platform and yelled for all to hear: 'Vee vant piss! All off us vant notink but piss!'

It was his finest hour.

Thirty-seven

They flew Aeroflop back to Moscow. Vasenka, Arnold and Ivanushka got to sit on seats. The two ducks shared one, next to the window, and their bills pressed against the glass as the plane skimmed high over the clouds.

'Life is wonderful! Imagine flying so high!' Vasenka exclaimed with awe. Arnold nodded knowingly.

Ivanushka had a middle seat, but his long neck allowed him to peer out of the window.

'Are those – are those people way down there?' he asked.

'Yes,' said Arnold wisely.

'But they look so – so small and harmless!'

'From a distance – yes, they do,' Arnold replied.

The professor sat in the aisle seat. The 'Fasten seat belts' light went out. The ducks unbuckled. Not Ivanushka. 'Not me! Not me! I'm scared. This is too high for me!' he said, fluttering his wings.

Flaffanoff appeared from the back of the plane. He was puffing on a long black Cuban cigar. 'Put that out!' commanded the stewardess. 'What do you think this is –

Pan Amerikan Airways? Lufthansa? Air France? Who do you think you are? Fidel Castro?'

She flapped a cloth napkin up and down, fanning the smoke upward. It curled along the ceiling. Flaffanoff flashed her his red lapel pin. The lady put down her napkin, hrumphed and returned to the rear of the plane. 'Just like a capitalist! Just like a capitalist!' she muttered to the passengers.

'Professor, join us in the back, for a smoke,' Flaffanoff said.

'I prefer it here,' the professor answered kindly.

Flaffanoff disappeared in a cloud of thick brown smoke.

'What have I wrought, Vasenka?' asked the professor, shaking his head sadly. 'What will become of all this, Arnold?' he asked over and over.

Arnold was silent.

'We all do what we must,' Ivanushka replied in a low voice.

'But what if it's for no purpose? Or, or worse – a bad purpose?'

'We all must do what we must.'

'It will come to no good! It's meddling in powers we don't understand.'

'Good will come of it,' Ivanushka replied wisely. 'Look, you worked out a way for ducks and geese to converse – with people too. Good will come of that!'

'But it's the other I anguish over – meddling with people's minds.'

'Good may come of that too.'

'Not with those people involved,' answered the professor, gesturing with his head towards the rear of the plane.

'Good may even come of that.'

'You're pretty wise for a goose,' the professor said, stroking Ivanushka's white feathers.

'And you're pretty considerate, for a human,' Ivanushka replied wisely

Thirty-eight

David left Moscow on a morning Air France flight. Sonya said goodbye to him outside the white double doors of the customs section at Sheremetevo Airport. She cried harder when David's hand passed from her cheek to her hair to the fur on her coat, and harder yet when the guard closed the door. Her cheek leaned against the concrete wall.

'My child, what is it? A death?' an old lady asked.
'No. But as final as death.'
'If it's not death, my dear, then there is hope.'
'There's no hope this time.' Sonya's tears flowed faster than before.

Thirty-nine

Sonya walked around Moscow that evening. Streets that had seemed warm, inviting, mysterious and beckoning when she walked with her David, were now plain, unfamiliar and cold.

Lights flickered from behind drawn lace curtains in upper storeys of buildings. Warm, intimate lights coming from shared spaces. Solid old buildings, like ships moored on either side of the street.

Mothers and fathers. Husbands and wives. Spaces not meant for her. Her David was gone. A world away, in America. They would never let him back into the country, she knew.

Forty

'My child, life goes on!' the professor told Sonya four days later, when she was still sobbing. She turned away, cried harder, and the professor waved his hands helplessly in the air.

'Come, my dearest, let's go for a walk.'

'I don't feel like walking now, Papa.'

'Walking always helps, precious. Please. I need one too.'

So they stepped out of their apartment in the Arbat section of Moscow and crossed Kalinin Prospekt. Down Suvorovsky and Vorovsky Streets, and finally down Gogolevsky. A dog barked as they walked past Number Seven, Gogolevsky Street.

'Beautiful evening for a walk,' said a man, stepping out of the evening fog. A tall man, with white skin that looked as if it were etched in stone, almost glistening in the dark evening light. He wore a black suit that seemed to disappear into the mist, a crisp shirt as white as his skin, and a narrow red tie. His collar stood high on his long neck.

'Beautiful evening for a walk,' he repeated. He looked like a foreigner, was dressed like a foreigner. His Russian, however, was correct. Overly precise, if anything. The man tipped his hat and bowed slowly as he spoke. A foreigner indeed. A gentleman.

'Yes, it is a beautiful evening,' the professor replied cautiously. This man could be a foreigner, a black-marketeer. Worse, a spy.

'You walk these spots often, Comrade Professor Proplavsky.'

A spy. A spy. The professor had never seen the man

before. Or anybody like him. Yet the stranger knew his name, addressed him familiarly, yet politely. There was something disarming, although awesome, in his manner.

'How comes it that – how do you know my name?'

'Memory! Filing! Organization!'

'You are a spy then?' the professor asked point-blank.

'Oh no, nothing that easy,' the stranger replied, laughing softly. 'Nothing that dishonest.'

'Then who are you?'

'I am what one expects to meet on a night like this.'

'You – you're a devil?' Sonya asked, taking her father firmly by the arm, as if to defend him.

'Oh, my!' The stranger laughed again, softly and politely. 'Such old categories and appellations! Do you prefer words like "Satan"? "Mephistopheles", perhaps?'

Across the street, a chorus of voices arose from one of the mansions. The strains of 'Oh Glorious, Glorious Baikal!' filled the street. It sounded almost like a hymn.

'There they go again. Tsk, tsk,' the stranger said. 'Oh!' He turned towards the professor and Sonya and extended his ungloved hand. 'My name is Woland. You can call me "Comrade Woland", if that is your desire.'

'Why are you here? What do you want?' the professor asked.

Woland laughed, a kindly laugh. 'Why are you here? That's more of a question. It takes a lifetime to find out sometimes!'

'What – what do you want from us?' Sonya asked, huddling next to her father.

'Such intriguing questions, Sonya! What do you want from me? Now that's a better question.' His eyes sparkled in the darkness, then lowered. 'You've been crying four days, Sonya. Your eyes are red, even in this darkness.'

'Lost love,' the professor said sadly.

'Lost love? Lost love?' Woland repeated, a hint of

amusement in his voice. 'There's no such thing as "lost love". It's a contradiction in terms.'

'But he's gone. He'll never come back!' Sonya protested, her voice both anguished and tearful.

'He may be gone, true. Physically gone, that is. But love! It's never gone. Never lost. It's one of the few things you can count on, in this crazy world,' he said. 'Except for drizzles in Moscow,' he added, holding his palm outward and upward. 'Not now. Please,' he said, looking upwards. 'Not now. Wait a bit, please!'

'Us?' the professor asked.

'No. Him.' Woland pointed upward, knowingly, winking. 'Communications problems sometimes,' he whispered.

Off to the side, Number Seven Gogolevsky Street, a squat building with two bay windows glowing in the darkness, looked like a fat, squatting cat.

Forty-one

'The Prezident of Amerika is coming to Moscow!' They shouted the words from rooftops, from basements, from vegetable stands and canned-goods stores. They broadcast them on radio, and the words were printed in thick, black letters on the front pages of *Pravda* and *Izvestia*.

'The Prezident of Amerika is coming to Moscow!' announced a sourpussed reporter on television. She screwed up her face with pride.

The Prezident of Amerika was coming to Moscow! From the way people acted on the streets, it looked like the second coming, end of the world, or worse, a scene from Gogol's *Government Inspector*.

A visiting collective-farm worker, minding his own

business (which at that moment involved looking for a prostitute), dropped his cigarette butt on to the sidewalk on Gorky Street.

'Shame on you, you tramp!' a babushka shouted, wagging her bony finger in his face. 'The Prezident of Amerika is coming to Moscow!'

Workers chopped up the pavement on Kalinin Prospekt. Rather, two women hacked away at the concrete while a dozen workers (they wore workers' uniforms, that is) stood around loafing and puffing on cigarettes. Traffic was backed up all the way around the Sadovaya.

'What the devil are you fools doing?' a red-faced cab driver yelled from his window. Behind him, a line of truck drivers leaned on their horns and shook their fists.

'The Prezident of Amerika is coming to Moscow!' the loafing workers replied, in chorus, while the ladies chopped at the pavement. The cab drivers and truck drivers nodded knowingly and stuck their heads back behind their windshields. As if it were the second coming.

And all along Moscow's main boulevards, workers painted the lower four storeys of all the buildings.

'Why are you vodka-heads only painting up to the fourth floor?' a man in a ripped T-shirt asked from his fifth-storey window.

'The Prezident of Amerika is coming to Moscow!'

'I know. I know. I heard it on television. But why are you bums painting only to the fourth floor?'

'The Prezident of Amerika will be in a covered car,' the painter answered, not looking up from his work.

'A covered car? So what? You don't make sense! Are you stupid?'

'No! You are! The prezident won't be able to see higher than the fourth-floor!'

'But I live on the fifth floor!' The man leaned out of the window, waving his arms like a bird. 'Paint my floor too!

The building will look ridiculous!'

'Paint shortage, you know!' the worker responded, not looking up. He dipped his brush daintily into his bucket, then held it out for the apartment dweller to see. 'Look! This stuff's almost like water as it is. If it rains, we'll all have yellow sidewalks!'

'To the devil with all of you!' the apartment dweller yelled as he slammed shut his window. Plaster dust fell down to the scaffold below.

'To the devil with you too, ingrate!' the worker shouted back, giving him the finger with the brush in his hand.

Forty-two

The whole city was crazy. 'The Prezident of Amerika is coming to Moscow!' It had a certain ring to it. A certain rhythm people caught on to. Mothers yelled it at kids crying in the park. Fathers repeated it as they pushed their sons into barber shops.

The Prezident of Amerika was coming to Moscow. Everyone heard it. Boys playing tape recorders too loud. Decadent girls wearing skirts too short. Kids chewing gum. A bureaucrat trying to pick up a prostitute in the Arbat, offering her only six roubles.

It was as if Lenin himself was putting on his overcoat and kapochka, getting ready to step out of the mausoleum and take a stroll around the city.

Forty-three

'Stand back, numskulls! Stand back!' the militiamen shouted at the crowds along Gorky Street. 'Haven't you seen a Prezident of Amerika before?'

'No,' was the usual reply.

'Well stand back anyway! Quit gawking like a bunch of roosters! Get back to work!'

'We're on break. Our bosses are here too.'

'Go about your business! Do something! Quit that gawking and rubbernecking! He's just a man! Just like the rest of us!'

'The man? Who in the devil's name cares about him? We're here to look at the cars!' a man with a big nose shouted, and the crowd nodded.

It was true. Black, sleek beasts, all of them (the cars). Thick tyres with white on the sides. Double headlights, like four-eyed monsters. Hoods longer than most Soviet cars altogether.

And inside, behind the long hoods, dashboards with stereo radios and cassette decks, blinkers and knobs of all sorts. And behind the dashboard, wide faces of smiling, well-fed capitalists. Car seats thicker than a Soviet sofa. These capitalists know how to drive around in style!

Then the longest car of them all came down Gorky (the street). Surrounded by motorcycles driven by Amerikan policemen with white bubble-hats, growling 'Ten-four! Ten-four!' into microphones with snakelike coiled cords. It was probably a CIA code.

All that fuss! Over a man with a thin wrinkled face, who sat dwarfed in the back seat of a limousine. The great comrade of capitalism himself. The Prezident of Amerika had come to Moscow.

He didn't nod at the crowds or crane his neck or even look out of the window. He didn't seem all that interested. They could have got by just painting the first storey.

The caravan squirmed like a nervous worm up the winding streets to the Kremlin.

Forty-four

'I don't want to sit by the wall! I want to sit by the window!' The Prezident of Amerika was not happy in Moscow, not even in the great Kremlin hall. He hadn't been happy in the Metropol Hotel that morning either. He asked for scrambled eggs with ketchup.

'So what is ketchup?' the head hotel chef asked.

'It's a sauce sort of thing. Tomato. A lot of salt,' Durfdovich explained, knowing everything about Amerika because he'd spent two months there.

'You want me to put something like that on an egg?' the chef asked incredulously. 'I quit!' With that, he threw down his apron, jumped on his paper hat and stormed out of the back door.

'I want a seat by the window!' the Prezident of Amerika repeated.

'That's my seat!' the premier bellowed back.

Poor Durfdovich stood in the middle. His big ears folded out at the top, like cabbages. He was born to be an interpreter.

'I want peace more than you do!' the great Soviet premier bellowed into Durfdovich's left ear, as if it were a megaphone.

'I want it more!' said the Prezident of Amerika, stamping his foot and yelling into Durfdovich's right ear.

Durfdovich ducked, twitching nervously. He'd been in scenes like this one before.

'We've always wanted peace!' the great comrade screamed louder, grabbing on to the tip of Durfdovich's ear. His entourage quaked as his voice reverberated throughout the room.

'You invaded Afghanistan!' the Prezident of Amerika shouted, jabbing Durfdovich in the shoulder.

Durfdovich ducked low on that one.

'You invaded South Vietnam!'

Durfdovich ducked lower.

'Stand up, you chicken-shit bastard!' the great comrade yelled at Durfdovich. 'I can't hear you down there!'

Durfdovich complied. Just in time to receive a jab from the skinny Prezident of Amerika.

'Poland!' the prezident yelled as he swung.

'Grenada!' the premier shouted, trying to poke the prezident in the eye. He hit Durfdovich's eye instead.

'Czechoslovakia!' Durfdovich ducked, and the prezident caught the premier right in the belly.

'Mozambique!' the premier shouted back, holding his stomach in pain.

It (the remark) caught the prezident off guard. 'Where the hell is Mozambique?' he asked his aide.

'I don't know, sir,' a skinny boy with pimples replied. 'I'm history, not geography.'

'You're a waste of time! That's what you are!'

Forty-five

The Moscow summit conference was not going well. While the leaders yelled at Durfdovich, reporters and photographers were pushing one another too, kicking and biting.

'Get out of my light, capitalist bastard!'

'Move your ugly tripod, you commie freak!'

Soon there was a pile of bodies on the carpet. Chunks of cameras and tripods littered the floor. The diplomats joined the fray and soon the great premier was on top of the prezident, who was on top of the defence minister, who was under a reporter.

The professor sat in the corner. Arnold and Vasenka peered out from the ends of the sofa. Ivanushka's beak stuck out from between the back-cushions.

'This isn't such a good example for us animals, you know,' Ivanushka said to the professor.

'It's not a good example for anyone or anything,' the professor replied.

'Now! It's time!' Barvingtov shouted to Flaffanoff from the bottom of the pile of squirming, punching bodies.

'Now, professor! The ring!' Flaffanoff shouted, fielding a kick to his shin. A reporter was biting at his other leg.

'You are crazy! Insane! All of you!' said the professor, shaking his head.

'Professor! Now! Someone'll be killed in this mess! Quick!' Flaffanoff yelled. As he shouted, a big capitalist hand came from behind and pushed his face down towards the carpet.

'The ring! The ring!' is what Flaffanoff probably yelled as he went down for the third time. It was hard to tell just what he was saying.

The professor shook his head, then shut his eyes and rubbed the ring. His finger rose in the air, spun around and stopped when it pointed towards the crowd.

'Kvak,' said Vasenka.

'What the hell – ?' asked the Prezident of Amerika, taking a jab from an Amerikan diplomat.

'Ducks! Geese!' the premier yelled to the prezident. 'You don't have ducks and geese in your cheap, sleazy America?'

'Of course we do, you communist runt! But our ducks don't go "kvak, kvak". I've never heard anything so dumb in all my life!'

'Quack,' said Arnold.

'That's better!' said the prezident. 'But animals at a summit meeting! You people are barbarians! Cavemen!'

'Ketchup on eggs! I heard about you! You're a barbarian!' the premier replied.

'You invaded Finland! 1939!'

'The Philippines! Spanish American War!' replied the great comrade, and the fighting continued. Diplomats swung curtain rods over their heads. Lawyers stabbed with pens and jabbed away with dented attaché cases.

'My brother's a dynamiter in Siberia!' Durfdovich yelled from the middle of the fracas. 'I want his job!'

A chair caught him on the back of the head.

Forty-six

Things were not going well at the Moscow summit conference. The Soviets were losing. The great premier had a bloody nose. Durfdovich was down for the count.

Through it all, the professor sat rubbing his ring. 'Extra

duty this time. Extra duty! I don't know if the power's strong enough for all this,' he repeated to himself, rubbing hard at the ring.

'Honk,' said Ivanushka, as if he'd hiccupped.

Heads turned. The room turned suddenly quiet. Everyone froze in motion, just where they were, as if it were a film and the projector had broken down. The prezident's mouth was stuck wide open. The premier was leaning back far on his heels, from the blow he'd just received. Leaning so far back that one puff of air would have blown him over. Photographers stood still, their hands stuck on shutters, and newsmen stood with pencils on pads.

No one made a sound. No one moved. It was like a Repin painting in the Tretiakov Gallery. Not bigger than life, however. Not smaller either, unfortunately.

Forty-seven

'Well! Well! Professor!' said a tall man in a black suit who came stepping across the room. He picked a piece of lint off his sleeve, then pointed towards the bodies frozen in motion. 'My! My! What have we wrought?'

'This is chaos!' the professor replied, pointing towards the pile of pugilist diplomats.

'That it is. That it is.' Woland stepped over two bodies. 'At least they're quiet for now. I can't hold them much longer, you know. It's a strain on things.' Woland wiped his brow with his white handkerchief. 'A strain. It upsets balances all over. You can imagine!'

'It's chaos! These people are crazy,' said the professor, shaking his head.

'They always have been, my friend.' Woland sighed.

'You've tapped into strange powers, professor. Trespassed, as it were.'

'I didn't know – they were powers, I thought. Powers for good, to do good.'

'Powers for good or evil, depending how they're used. Powers that manipulate other humans! Tsk, tsk. That's reserved for higher beings.' Woland pointed towards the ceiling.

'Powers for good. But look what they've tried to do with it!' The professor pointed towards Flaffanoff and Barvingtov, frozen in the heap of bodies.

'They're crazy,' Woland replied. 'All of them. Those kind couldn't do good if you gave them directions and paid them.'

'Well, why don't you do something?' the professor asked, almost accusingly.

Woland crossed his arms in front of him. 'Free will, you know.' He shook his head and rolled his eyes upward. 'I warned them it wouldn't work – ages ago, I warned them.'

'But can't you hold them in check, control it?'

'My, professor! We sound like a Marxist today!'

'But – but prevent this chaos? If you can?'

'People get what they deserve, my friendly professor. They get what they ask for, even if they don't know they're asking for it.'

'But this! This is chaos! Can't they learn? Can't we teach them a lesson?'

'Probably not,' Woland replied, sighing, looking down at his watch. 'It is not permitted – usually.' He dusted off his shoulder. 'Tell you what. Let's try anyway!'

'Can I help?'

'Anxious to play God, or Marx? No. It's better for you and your friends to go away from here. I'll try. You go back to the laboratory. Stay there, in that blessed solitude, for twenty-four hours. Agreed?'

'Agreed!' The professor gathered up his coat and hat. 'Come, Arnold. Come, Vasenka. Come, Ivanushka. Let's leave this chaos, this abyss. Abyss abissynum vocat.'

'Latin, how fitting!!' Woland exclaimed. 'Latin and Russian! How fitting!'

The professor walked across the wide hall, his little feet barely touching the carpet. Arnold and Vasenka followed, waddling, while Ivanushka took up the rear, his orange beak nodding forward as he walked. The room was so quiet you could hear the slap-slap of webbed feet on the parquet floor.

Forty-eight

The train station was crowded, and the evening Red Arrow Express from Leningrad to Moscow was scheduled to leave on time, of course.

'All comrade-passengers on board!' said the anonymous voice coming over the speakers. Misha and Mary hurried along the platform. Their car was near the end, and the train would leave in three minutes.

'I look forward to meeting your mother,' Mary said nervously, panting as they rushed past the train cars.

'Halt!' It was a threatening male voice. Three thick-necked men in leather coats stepped out from a train door and blocked their path.

'Please! We'll miss the train,' Mary said in Russian.

'Misha?' the man in the middle asked. 'Mikhail Bombeev?'

'Yes. That's my name,' Misha replied, with resignation in his voice.

'You can't leave Leningrad,' said the man in the middle, grinning. 'It is not permitted.'

'Why not?'

'Soviet trains are for workers, not parasites.'

'Come on, Misha. Let's go back!' Mary pleaded, tugging at his arm.

'No,' he replied firmly. 'We'll make a stand here. I am not a parasite,' he said firmly, looking the man in the middle squarely in the eye. 'I am a poet.'

'A poet, is he?' the middle man asked of his two companions. 'A poet, is it?' He jabbed Misha in the chest. 'Are you a member of the writers' union?'

'No.'

'Then you're not a poet. You're a parasite.'

'I am a poet,' Misha repeated, in the same quiet tone as before.

'Who says?'

'I do.'

The man laughed. 'You're not in the union? Where is your union card?'

'I have none.'

'Then you're not a poet. Documents make the man, you know.'

'I am a poet. Please let me pass. The train is starting to move.'

Mary stepped forward, her eyes flashing at the man in the middle. 'I am an American citizen. Here's my passport. Please let us pass, or I'll file a complaint with the militia. With the American Embassy too.'

The man said nothing. He stepped to the side, and Misha and Mary continued on their way.

Forty-nine

'My son, you are so thin! Here! Eat. Herring. Biscuits. Some sausage. Here!'

'I'm not hungry, Mama.'

'Eat, my child. You must hold together body and soul.' Sofinya turned towards Mary. 'He thinks only of the soul. But, my word! He must feed himself too!'

Fifty

Mary and Sofinya became fast friends, and both cared for Misha.

Mary talked with Sofinya about books she'd read in college. Poetry, John Donne. Ezra Pound. Verses she remembered. Lines that now acquired new meaning. Gerard Manley Hopkins. She tried translating 'The Windhover' for Sofinya, who sat silently in awe, her eyes watering.

Late on rainy evenings, Sofinya told Mary stories. Russian fairy tales. Things she'd told Misha when he was a boy. Baba Yaga, the witch who rode in a mortar and steered with a pestle. Russalka, the sea maiden. Sadko, the merchant. The invisible city of Kitezh. And when she finished one of her stories, she pulled out tiny enamelled Palekh boxes that retold the tales in bright colours.

Fifty-one

'Mary and I are in love,' Misha told his mother as they sat in the kitchen of her tiny apartment.

'In love! A wonder! A miracle, children!' Sofinya wiped a tear from her eye with the tip of her apron. 'Care for it! Nuture it! Preserve it!'

The samovar hummed in the background, and a cat miaowed in the courtyard.

'Mary wants to live here – in Leningrad, I mean,' Misha said.

Sofinya smiled as she poured the tea. 'Wonderful! An enchanted city!'

'I'll find work, so Misha can write,' Mary said. 'I can translate, or teach English.' The excitement faded from her voice. 'If I can stay here.'

'They won't let you?' Sofinya asked.

'They – the Americans – won't let me stay.'

'Why not, child?'

'They say I've worked in sensitive areas – security. I must wait two years.' Mary's head drooped in sadness as she spoke.

Fifty-two

The professor and his entourage walked out of the Kremlin, down the long sloping pathway across from the Menage, and back across Red Square. They did not look back. It was good that they didn't.

It started right in the great hall of the Kremlin. The

freeze-frame film came to life slowly, as if in slow-motion. Then it speeded up, to normal speed, then faster and faster. Chairs flew towards the chandeliers. The Prezident of Amerika jumped on the great premier's stomach. 'You blood-thirsty heathen!'

The premier bit the prezident's finger and flipped him over like a sausage on a griddle. The premier was now on top. 'Capitalistic warmonger! Enemy of the people!'

Bodyguards and security men joined the fray. A Soviet cameraman hit his American counterpart over the head with a 'Zenit' foto-apparat. Its lens dangled like a cuckoo in a sick clock. An Amerikan in a polka-dot suit took wide swings with his tripod. Glasses smashed. The Russians yelled 'Oi' and the Amerikans yelled 'Ouch!'

The chaos was not limited to the great hall of the Kremlin for long. A skinny TASS reporter flew out of a window, head first, and landed on a fat lady, who started hitting him with her purse. 'Masher! Is nothing sacred? Right here in the Kremlin! It's a sin! A Marxist sin, it is!'

'Holy mother! You have bricks in that cursed purse!' he yelled as his hands flew up to protect his face.

'I wish to the devil I did, you pervert!' the lady replied, taking another swing. It missed – the jumper that is – and landed right smack in the face of an innocent bystander.

'Why? – hmmmpff,' was all the man could say as the purse sailed into his face. He took a wild swing that missed the lady but hit the side of a Volga sedan. The fat driver stepped calmly out of the car, looked at the dent in his fender, opened his trunk, and went chasing after the man with a tyre iron. When he couldn't catch up, he threw the tyre iron forward, and it went singing dizzily through the air. It missed its target, but caught the window of a bus.

'This bus is state property, you – you criminal!' The driver slammed on his brakes, stepped out of his bus, grabbed a skillet from a pedestrian (as luck would have it, they were on sale that day in Skillet Shop Number Thirty-four, just down the street from where the tyre iron met the bus windshield). The flying skillet slid to a landing on a counter in Fish Market Number Seventy-five, after having passed through a plate-glass window and grazing four shoppers. Three of the four shoppers started beating the bus driver over the head with dead sturgeons.

In the process, a pushcart was knocked over, and its Armenian proprietor started jumping up and down. 'My pirozhki! Ruined! Ruined My push-cart – she is ruined too!' He was jumping up and down all over his pirozhki. Then he jumped on the fingers of a man down for the count with a dead sturgeon beating away at him. And soon, people were pelting one another with greasy pirozhki.

Things might have stopped there if someone hadn't broken the window of the record shop, because then people started sailing records through the air like deadly boomerangs that wouldn't return. A lady walking her dog was smacked in the face with the death scene from *Boris Godunov*, the great Fyodor Chaliapin performing. A militiaman rushing to restore order was hit with the cutting edge of *The Dance of the Sugar-plum Fairy*, Moscow Radio Orchestra Number Seven. A short man raising a brick high in the air was knocked over by the Osipov Balalaika Ensemble, *Favourites of the Baikal Region*.

Like a stone dropped into a stagnant puddle, the chaos spread out from the Kremlin. Up Gorky Street. Into the Arbat. Out to the Sadovaya Ring. Past Novodevichi one way, Andronnikov the other way. A deputy minister got into a fist-fight with his grandmother in front of Holy Trinity Cathedral. Some fool climbed up Saint Ivan's bell tower, and soon all Moscow was ringing the bells. It was like 1812 all over again, without the fire, without Napoleon. No Tchaikovsky, except for the militiaman hit with the sugar-plum fairy. People rushed out or tumbled out on to the streets. Some fell, or were thrown from windows.

Television screens blinked, just at the point where the sour-faced lady announced, 'And in the decadent West today, riots broke out in . . .'

No one ever found out where. Television screens went blank all over Moscow, all over the RSFSR, as a matter of fact. Radio Moscow lost its signal, just at the high point of its evening interview programme: 'How, comrade, did you manage to increase production in your prophylactic factory by 400 per cent in one month?' The answer may never be known. An annoying hum came over all Moscow's radio sets. The station went off the air. The chaos spread everywhere.

Somehow, it even got inside the hallowed halls of the Bolshoi Ballet. First, there was shuffling and scuffling behind the curtain. Then a dead fish came sailing across the stage. The lead dancer turned to get a better look. Unfortunately, he lost his balance and, even more unfortunately, he was holding Sleeping Beauty at the time. The beauty, no longer asleep, plopped to the floor, then got up and hit the dancer with a loose floorboard. While yanking at the floorboard, she knocked over a whole section of ladies in tutus on their tiptoes. They fell like dominoes, each of them punching the one in front, except the first one, who went after the stage manager for reasons unrelated.

The audience joined in. First the front rows, then the entire ground floor. Then the *belle étage* and soon, not to be outdone simply for paying less or bribing less for tickets, all the balconies.

Lights all over the city went out. Trolleys stopped. The metro stopped. The howling and punching went on all night long.

The world (Moscow, at least) would never be the same.

The professor peered out of his third-floor window cautiously, looking down over Bashmakovsky Street and the chaos beyond. 'Come, Arnold. Come, Vasenka. Come, Ivanushka. Let's retire for the evening.' He shut the laboratory windows one by one, and the steady roar from the city below gradually became more muffled.

An hour later the chaos continued, spreading to the dachas and peat bogs around Moscow. The professor slept at his desk. His cheek lay flat across an open book. Ivanushka buried his head under his left wing, and dozed next to the professor's lamp. Arnold and Vasenka crouched in the corner near the radiator. Their feathers rose and fell, rose and fell, softly and evenly as they slumbered.

Fifty-three

A cool evening breeze blew off the Gulf of Finland, up the Neva River, and forced its way down Leningrad's streets and canals. Mary walked along the river from the Winter Palace, past the square, past Gogol Street, up Nevsky to the Cathedral of Our Lady of Kazan.

She walked alone. The militia had picked Misha up again last night, their first evening back in Leningrad. 'For questioning,' the man said. It was the same man who had blocked their way at the train station. Misha would be back by morning, probably. Then they'd question the friends who gave him food and a place to sleep. It was their usual routine.

Mary walked behind the cathedral, following the jagged path of the Moika Canal. It was dark, especially after the bright lights of Nevsky Prospekt. She paused on the bridge running across the canal. The low-slung footbridge, with two lions at each end.

Such a beautiful city. Such an ethereal, unworldly city. If only she could live there, with Misha. She'd care for him. He could write his verses, in peace. A chill wind blew across the bridge. It would be winter soon. Her visa expired in December.

Swirls of black mist rose from over the murky water below. The fog had rolled in, covering most of the city, muffling lights and muzzling sounds. Mary could hardly see a metre in front of her.

'Darkness. We're good at it here.' It was a man's voice, cutting through the fog. Precise. Russian. A touch of a foreign accent. German perhaps. The mist curled upwards from the canal in a slow spiral, and the black water became visible. A fish jumped.

'Darkness. Who knows what happens – what can happen – in darkness?' The mysterious, foreboding words made her tremble. She looked to her left. Out of the fog, or out from the fog stepped a man. Tall. Black suit. Red tie nearly glowing in the darkness. A crisp white shirt with a tall collar tight against his neck. Ivory-white skin. Deep-set, glowing eyes. A white scarf, silk probably, wrapped neatly around his neck, its ends tucked flat into his coat. He held a walking-stick. Its top glowed as if reflecting light off something.

'Yes, it's dark tonight,' she said bravely. 'There's no moon.'

'Oh, there's always a moon. It's just that sometimes you don't see it. How human! To think that something doesn't exist because you can't see it.'

Just then, the fog seemed to part, and a hole appeared in the clouds off towards the river. A full moon showed. The man nodded, and his smile shone in the moonlight. Clouds blew past, and the moon disappeared.

'Who – who are you?' Mary asked.

'I am sometimes called "the force called evil that sometimes does good".' The man wiped the moisture off the tip of his walking-stick. 'That's a rather long name. A bit outdated too. You can call me "Woland". That's less outdated.'

Fifty-four

Moscow looked as bad as a drunk on New Year's Day morning.

All along its streets, Muscovites filed by in silence, not looking up, not looking off to the side. No one spoke.

Workers cleared the streets, loading dump trucks high with broken furniture, dented refrigerators, bent tyre irons, squashed pirozhki, shards of glass, pieces of phonograph records and dead sturgeons. Cranes hoisted trolleys back on to the tracks. Caretakers and shopkeepers shovelled trash off their walkways and aisles.

All went about in silence. Dogs howled in the distance. Ravens crowed.

Fifty-five

The Moscow chaos followed the Amerikan Prezident home. When his aeroplane landed near Vashinkton, screaming reporters craned their necks and jostled one another in the terminal. It was for naught.

The prezident hopped right out of his plane into a helicopter that had plopped right down on the tarmac. The helicopter angled upwards like an overweight dragonfly, and soon the Prezident of Amerika was walking across his neatly trimmed White House grass. The big fan on top of the helicopter uprooted plants and knocked the hats off reporters. A toupé sailed off towards the horizon.

'Mister Prezident!' all the newspeople shouted, trying to get his attention. A thick red rope with two square-shouldered marines held them back off the neat White House grass.

'What was the outcome of your secret Moscow talks?' they shouted from their barricade.

The prezident smiled and lifted two fingers into the air to form a 'V'.

'Mister Prezident! Will peace break out?'

The prezident paused, looking towards the newspeople. 'I'll say this about that.' He rubbed the bite marks on his knuckles. 'We are clearly on top of the situation.'

The newspeople looked puzzled, unsatisfied.

'We were on the bottom,' the Prezident of Amerika added. 'Then we were on top.'

'Were there any new initiatives?' asked a skinny man wearing round glasses and a rubber rain hat.

'We hit them with some new proposals – yes!' He grinned a wide, triumphant grin.

A clamour arose among the reporters and cameramen. 'Mister Prezident! Mister Prezident!' They all shouted in unison, so the 'Mister Prezident' part was discernible. Nothing else was.

'Mister Prezident!' a jowl-faced lady yelled, jabbing a microphone forward. Her voice was lower than the others, so it was heard. 'What about your prostate operation?'

The prezident humpfed.

'Show us the scar!' the lady demanded.

The prezident lifted his middle finger high into the air and frowned unkindly at the lady reporter.

'Show us the scar!' she repeated. Others joined in, chanting, waving their microphones and notepads. 'Show us the scar! Show us the scar!'

'No!' said the Prezident of Amerika with authority.

'LBJ showed us his!' the lady yelled, and soon it became the chant. 'LBJ showed us his! LBJ showed us his!'

'That was a gallbladder scar!' the Prezident of Amerika said in a huff, stomping into the White House. The security men slammed shut the door.

Fifty-six

The chaos spread all over Vashinkton, like hot lard across a piece of limp Amerikan bread.

The streets of the capital were jammed with people beating one another over the head with signposts and clubs.

'Pro-life! Pro-life!' a frenzied woman yelled in front of a building that said 'Department of Justice'. A dozen old men in black robes slunk through a side entrance, their heads bent low to the ground.

'Kill the bastards!' the lady yelled, pointing towards the old men.

'Kill the bastards! Kill the bastards!' went the chant from the crowd.

'Aids to the contras!' a lady in the middle of a second bevy of yellers screamed.

'No, dummy! Aid to the contras! Aids to the gays!' a skinny man with a squeaky voice screamed. 'Move over anyway!' he shouted. 'We were here first!' he shouted as he whacked her over the head with his picket sign.

'No! We were here first!' a short, fat man yelled, waving and swooping his sign high in the air. 'Kill the Secular Humanists and Other Commies!' he chanted.

A new group of people with angry expressions marched

down the street. 'Get out of here, weirdos! We were here first!'

'We were here first!' said the pro-lifers.

'We were here first!' said the aids to the contras.

'We've been here thirty-five years!' a snarling old lady in the front of the new group shouted. 'USA out of the UN!' she chanted, and her followers followed.

'Get out of our way with your ugly fucking signs!' the ladies from another group yelled, charging in from the rear. The street was getting crowded. The signs these angry ladies carried said 'Put God back into public schools!' and 'Darwin's an ape!'

'Don't yell so loud, you pinkos!' shouted the USA-out-of-the-UN group.

'Drag the fucking commies out into the light of day!' shouted yet another group. They wore white sheets and hoods with slanting eyeslits.

Whistles blew and motorcycles roared. Then the police marched down from three directions, with shields that flapped in front of them. They wore gasmasks that made them look like grasshoppers, and carried long sticks. 'Order! Order! We must have order!' They looked like a plague of locusts descending on the Department of Justice.

'Go to hell!' all the groups shouted, finally agreeing with one another on something.

'Disperse! We order you to disperse!' a fat policeman with a black bullhorn commanded.

'Homes for the poor! Homes for the homeless!' yet another group chanted, waving sticks at the policemen.

'Go home!' the fat policeman yelled.

There was shoving and pushing. It was worse than People's Meat Market Number Thirty-four on monthly delivery day. Worse than the Moscow subway at the start of a three-day holiday.

Fists flew. Signs came crashing down on heads. Banners

fell to the ground, and policemen waved clubs high in the air.

Horns honked all over Vashinkton. Dogs howled. Cats wailed. Cars collided and buses stalled in traffic.

The Moscow chaos had descended on Vashinkton.

No one noticed.

Fifty-seven

As if nothing had happened, Radio Moscow went back on the air two days after the chaos. They had a hot story. A watch factory had over-fulfilled its quota again. The first batch would work eventually, the factory chairman promised.

Then there was a news flash. People's Benevolent Shoe Factory had come out with a stylish number. High heels for women. The cast-iron heels would last for ever, as soon as they figured out how to attach them to the shoes.

'There will be plenty of railroad cars for the harvest,' the minister of trolleys, trains and other vehicles on tracks reported.

'There will be no harvest,' the minister of agriculture told listeners sadly. 'The planters didn't get their seeds on time. Then the tractors stalled, and parts were not available.'

Then there was another bulletin. The people had a new minister of agriculture. Comrade Puntovich, formerly minister of culture and water aquatics. A new minister of tractors, bulldozers and spare parts too. Comrade Xlebovich, the former minister of agriculture.

All over Moscow, television sets turned back on. The weather would be clear over much of the country. Part forty-three of *Our Glorious Motherland* would be aired that evening, having been delayed two days because of technical difficulties. 'The Red Army will win the war,' the announcer assured the viewers.

Trains departed and arrived on time. And, at just the right moment, the honour guards stomped out of the Ivan Bell Tower, marched along the Kremlin wall, and reached the mausoleum just as the first bell peeled. As had been planned. As always had been planned. Everything was in order.

'What did you do the night before last?' Muscovites asked one another in casual tones.

'Oh, nothing much,' was the usual reply. 'Just a normal, boring night. Nothing on television to speak of, of course.'

No one would speak of it. The chaos. Perhaps no one remembered. Like a man who forgets what he did the night he was drunk. People scratched their heads and picked their noses pensively, as if they wanted to recall something, but couldn't remember what.

Would the strange events of that previous night go unrecorded, unremembered? Had something happened that would remain outside history? Beyond recollection? Outside the collective consciousness, as Marx or Engels might say?

Someone had wiped the slate clean. Almost.

Fifty-eight

The world would never be the same. Days later, Moscow and Vashinkton still looked like battle zones. A disorder never before seen in Moscow.

'What – what happened here?' a puzzled collective farmer asked as he stared at a ten-metre-high pile of rubble on Gorky Street. 'We don't have messes like that in

Tula, comrades!'

'What do you mean, "what happened"?' a surly workman asked, poking his shovel towards the nosey farmer from Tula.

'This rubble. This mess. Is Moscow always so – so disorderly?' the collective-farm worker asked shyly.

'It's subbotnik, dummy! A clean-up day!'

The man from Tula frowned.

'A workers' sabbath!' said the man, pushing a pile of broken bricks with his shovel.

'But that paint dripping off buildings. Those yellow puddles in the gutter. Broken glass. Boarded-up windows!'

'A clean-up – that's all!' said the worker, with a look on his face that said, 'Mind your own business, dirty peasant!'

A row of drab green dump trucks lurked about the city, their engines grumbling, their drivers dozing at the wheel.

Fifty-nine

The professor picked his way up Bashmakovsky Street, stepping around broken glass and pirozhki hardened like rocks. An uprooted tree blocked his path.

'Good morning, professor!' A man in a black suit and a bright red tie waved politely from across the street. His feet crushed over bits of broken glass as he picked his way across the street. A dump truck zipped past, its horn blaring.

'Quite a mess here!' the man in the black suit said.

'The world has never seen anything like it!' the professor replied.

'Oh, the world has seen plenty of chaos. This is a light dose. You should see the capitalist West sometimes, professor!'

Woland's foot made a small circle over bits of broken black plastic. 'This mess will be gone in three days. Mark my words. Three days! It will seem like a miracle. All Moscow is hard at work. That's a miracle in itself.'

'No one will remember what happened?' the professor asked.

'No one will remember. Unfortunately,' Woland replied.

'Is that so unusual?'

'Such chaos! Such pandemonium! And no one – not a soul – will remember?'

'To forget lessons of history? That's not so unusual, is it? You humans do it all the time.'

They walked arm in arm down Bashmakovsky. 'Will no one remember?' the professor asked.

'Only if someone writes it down.'

'Someone must! Me! I'll write it all down!'

'No, professor,' Woland replied. 'You've done your part. You deserve a rest.'

Sixty

Two weeks after the chaos night, Vasenka and Arnold frolicked in a corner of the laboratory on the third floor of the Tikvin Institute. The professor sat at his desk, writing. His head leaned low over the paper. One hand held his glasses. The other hand held a pencil that scratched back and forth across the paper.

Ivanushka stood on the top of the desk, off to the side. His neck bent low over the paper. 'What are you writing, professor?'

'The results of my experiments. I must record what happened.'

'You people are so strange,' Ivanushka said.

'The world is strange,' the professor replied, scratching away at the paper.

'Yes. But you humans are strangest of all!'

The professor looked up from his papers. 'True. True. Why do you think it's so, my friend?' He stroked the goose's smooth, long back.

'Humans stand up too straight,' Ivanushka replied. 'All that strain! Too far from the ground! It's enough to make anyone dizzy – fighting gravity like that all the time.'

'That's true, probably,' the professor remarked, handing the goose a biscuit.

'Worse,' Ivanushka continued, swallowing.

'What do you mean?'

'Their eyes are too close together. They point forward too much!'

'What's the problem with that, my feathery friend?'

'Look at us geese,' Ivanushka replied. 'Our eyes are off to the sides. We see more around us. Our necks let us look all around too – see!' Ivanushka demonstrated. 'We see more. Not just where we're going. Where we are too.'

'Where you are too,' the professor repeated pensively. 'Would that we saw where we are!'

'And remembered what happened,' Ivanushka replied.

'Someone must write it down – all of it,' said the professor, turning back to his notes.

Sixty-one

The curtains in the third-floor laboratory fluttered in the cool night breeze. They'd been wafting back and forth all night. Up flat against the screen, then rustling back and forth restlessly. Then back up flat against the screen again.

The professor read at his desk, his goose-neck lamp

hovering over the pages like an ever-watchful eye. Arnold and Vasenka strolled around the laboratory, picking at lint on the carpet. Next to the professor's chair, Ivanushka had laid a book flat out against the floor. He honked quietly to himself, flipping the pages with his beak. His neck curled gracefully as his head turned to and fro, his eyes following the lines on the page.

The curtains stirred, more than before, and their bottom edges fluttered straight out in the breeze, but there was no breeze. The room was still.

'Good evening, my friends! Good evening!' A deep, melodious voice. A man appeared as if from nowhere. Wearing a black suit and a bright red tie.

'Such a tranquil scene – so out of character with this century!' the man said, looking about the room. 'What are you reading, professor?' His intonation said he already knew.

'Goethe,' the professor replied, looking up from his book. 'About Doctor Faustus. I'll never understand.'

'Things are different now,' the tall man said, smiling. '"Times have changed," as the saying goes.'

'What do you mean?' The professor looked up at the visitor with curiosity. Ivanushka did likewise.

'Those neat distinctions – gods and devils – they've gone by the board. Forces of darkness, forces of light – things got too confused.'

'So?' The professor urged his visitor on.

'So we don't follow the old categories any more. Agreements have been negotiated. Signed even.'

'What agreements?'

Woland pointed up towards the ceiling. 'Agreements. Contracts. We try to co-operate now – stay out of each other's way.'

'I should throw away Goethe then?'

'Oh no, my dear professor, certainly not! Literature

always has its messages.'

Woland took three steps towards the professor and motioned for Arnold and Vasenka to draw near. The curtains now hung motionless in the stilled room.

'And now, my twentieth-century Moscow friends,' Woland began slowly, almost wearily. 'It's time for our reckoning.' There was a twinkle in his left eye, something of a glint in his right eye. A far-away look.

'A reckoning?' asked the professor.

'Settling accounts. Do not worry. You've all done quite well. I am pleased.' Woland pointed towards the ceiling. 'So is he, I might add.'

There was a bolt of lighting and a clap of thunder, although the night was clear and the stars visible.

Woland sat down on a tall stool, the tails of his black coat barely touching the floor. His fingered a Bunsen burner on the counter off to his side. 'Time for the reckoning.' His fingers flicked across the tip of the burner and, as if by magic, a blue flame appeared. 'Arnold and Vasenka, step up here, please. Towards me. Don't shiver. Don't be afraid.'

They complied, waddling cautiously forward.

'It's up the ladder for you two. You have done well, my lads!'

The ducks looked at each other inquisitively, their beaks slanting off in opposite directions.

Poof! There was a strong flash from the Bunsen burner, then a thick orangeish smoke like phosphorus filled the room. The smoke curled towards the ceiling, then snaked out through the window.

'Instant evolution!' Woland proclaimed. 'A la Marx and Engels, my friends!'

Where Arnold and Vasenka had been crouching – well, now stood two tall, handsome gentlemen. Two princes, strong and handsome, perhaps of foreign extraction. One with blond hair and blue eyes. The other with brown, wavy hair and deep-set hazel eyes. Both with wide, angular shoulders and finely chiselled features. Deep baritone voices.

'Behold Arnold! Behold Vasenka!' Woland proclaimed, raising his hands in the air. 'Behold my new assistants! My right-hand men!'

'Right-hand men? Why?' the professor asked.

'Who ever heard of right-hand ducks? Come, my assistants, there's work to be done!' Woland led the way towards the window.

'What – what about me?' Ivanushka's timid voice came from the top of the professor's desk. He'd tried to hide behind the lamp when the puff of orange smoke filled the room. His voice trembled. His feathers quivered. He looked down sadly at his orange webbed feet. 'What about me?'

'You, my friend, have a mission.'

'Why?'

'It's karma, my friend. It's hard to explain – it would take years.'

'But why not me? Arnold and Vasenka – I'm happy for them. But why not me? I've been a good goose?'

'Karma, my friend.'

'Was I – have I been a bad goose?'

'A good goose, but you were a man once,' Woland replied.

'Yes? Is that so bad?'

'Not necessarily. But in your case, yes, it was bad. You were an attorney. A prosecutor.'

'That explains it!' said Ivanushka, looking down at his webbed feet as if they were shoes somebody had forced him to wear.

'Not only that,' Woland continued. 'It gets worse!'

Ivanushka shuddered, blinking his little eyes.

'You were a politician once.'

'Oh no!'

'Oh yes! Why, just this past life you were an Amerikan. In the Nixon administration.'

'Oh no!'

'Oh yes! And worse, before that, you were an anarchist.'

'A terrorist?'

'No, thankfully, or you'd be back down with the spiders, or worse, insurance salesmen,' Woland said, smiling kindly. 'You were a theoretical anarchist, it was called. An associate of Prince Peter Kropotkin.'

'Was that bad?' Invanushka asked innocently.

'You helped form "The International League of Anarchists". Imagine! Such a contradiction in terms! It defies all logic – even Marxist logic. For that, you must pay, unfortunately.'

'I'm sorry I did all that!'

'I know, my friend. I wish I could help you.' He pointed towards the ceiling. 'I can't. It's not my department. I'm very sorry.'

'So – so what is my punishment?' Ivanushka strained his neck forward and his eyes blinked shut, as if trying to block out with his eyes what his goose ears would hear.

'Think of it as a mission, not as punishment. You must tell the story.'

'This story?'

'Yes. All of it.'

'But how?'

'Honestly. Completely. Without embellishment.'

'No – I mean how? I mean, mechanically how?'

'You'll work it out, my friend. There's a nice typewriter downstairs.' Woland winked as he put one foot up on the window sill. 'Come, Arnold! Come, Vasenka! There's work to be done!'

'Wait!' It was the professor's voice. 'Comrade Woland, I

– I –' He stood up from his chair. 'I ask nothing for myself. I do what I must – but my daughter – Sonya. Could she not be helped? Couldn't you do something?'

Woland waved his arm and his cloak wrapped itself around his shoulder. 'Things will work out by themselves. They always do, one way or the other. We're not allowed unlimited meddling any more, you know. Things will work out, believe me. With a little help from us. Just a little. When it's required.'

Woland winked, and stepped up on to the sill. A flash, then orange smoke. When it cleared, Woland and his two handsome assistants had vanished.

Sixty-two

'Things will work out on their own, Ivanushka! Did you hear him say that? Things will work out on their own.' The professor patted his glum companion on the top of his head.

'I can't write! I don't know how, professor. It seems hopeless.'

'It's never hopeless. Let us begin! Let us go down to the typewriter!'

The pair headed for the stairway.

'I wish I could walk faster, professor. This waddling's no fun!'

'Come, Ivanushka. No more complaining! Let us begin!'

'You'll – you'll help me, professor?'

'Every way that I can, my friend. Every way that I can.'

Sixty-three

A night light burned on the first floor of the institute. Sofinya Haroldovna sat at her desk, reading.

'Working late, Sofinya Haroldovna?'

'No, professor. Reading. It's blessed quiet here in the evening.'

'That it is. What are you reading?'

'Poetry.'

'Pushkin?'

'No. My son's. Misha's a poet.'

'Then read us some, aloud. Please.'

The professor sat down, and Ivanushka curled up at his side. Sofinya bent the lamp low, and started reading.

Sixty-four

The professor and Ivanushka marvelled at what they heard. Beautiful lyrics. Music to the ears.

'Come. Let us go up to the laboratory, and I shall make us some tea!' said the professor. They headed for the elevator, Ivanushka trailing behind, still shaking his head in despair.

Zip! Halfway up, the elevator jammed, stuck between floors. It wouldn't move.

'Life is crazy lately – crazier than before,' said Sofinya. 'Everything's topsy-turvy.'

'We must do the best we can. The best we can,' the professor said, patting Ivanushka on the head.

The professor and Sofinya sat down on the floor.

Ivanushka curled up in Sofinya's lap, his head following the lines that she read from Misha's poems.

Sixty-five

They were stuck in the French elevator for more than two hours. When Sofinya finished reading, she talked about her life and about her son, Misha. The professor talked about his life and about his daughter, Sonya.

'Would that they could find a way around their difficulties!' said the professor.

'Love conquers all!' said Sofinya, and the professor nodded in agreement.

By the end of the second hour, there was another couple in love. An old, widowed professor. An old, widowed typist. They kissed.

On the first floor, a man in a black cape wiped the dust from his hands. 'Tsk, tsk. French elevators,' he said, examining the wires poking out from the wall panel. 'They should have ordered German.'

The man pushed in on the dusty red knob. The elevator jerked, then softly and gently it rose to the third floor.

Sixty-six

It was dark in the Tikvin Institute, save for a small lamp on Sofinya's desk. Ivanushka stood atop her chair, his neck craned forward, his beak aimed sideways at the keyboard. 'These keys are so close together! I can hardly hit just one!'

'Just do the best you can, my friend!' said the professor.

'I'll help – I'll show you how,' Sofinya added, leading the

goose by his beak towards the right keys.

'But the story. The whole story!' said Ivanushka in despair, shaking his head wide from side to side.

'Just start at the beginning,' Sofinya said. 'And stop when you get to the end.'

Tap. Tap. His beak poked away at the keys. 'Take it page by page,' said Sofinya.

'It hurts!' said Ivanushka, rubbing his beak against the side of the black Smit-Korona.

'You'll get used to it. My fingers hurt at first too,' Sofinya said.

Tap. Tap. The heavy black carriage jerked two spaces to the left. 'It will take a long time – such a very long time!'

'Make every word count,' said the professor.

Tap. Tap. Tap-tap-tap. Ring!

Sofinya showed him how to work the carriage return.

'The world would never be the same.' She read aloud his first line, and patted him proudly on the back.

Tap. Tap. Tap-tap-tap. Ring! Ivanushka pushed the Smit-Korona carriage back to the right with the side of his head. 'What about the parts I don't know?'

'They'll come to you,' said the professor. 'Just watch for them. It's called "inspiration".'

Sixty-seven

'This is the line waiting to get into the line over there!' a grouchy old lady yelled at a man who had just stepped into the crowded room.

Murvella Petrovna, the clerk, obviously wasn't having a good day. Few government clerks ever have a good day, but this day was worse than most for this particular clerk. What with stacks of papers sliding every which way on the counter. Hot and humid. The windows painted shut. The old fan, caked with dust, wasn't working again. Hundreds of smelly citizens crammed into the small reception space of the passport application office, pounding greasy fists on the counter, waving wrinkled papers in their dirty palms.

'Pushy comrades! Smelly citizens! I can only take care of one at a time!' the old clerk shouted. 'One at a time! Quiet! I can't concentrate!'

'One at a time?' asked an old woman in line. 'Who are you taking care of now then? You're reading *Pravda*!'

'All of us have a duty to be informed, young lady,' said Murvella Petrovna, not looking up from her paper. If she had looked up, she may have noticed that the woman she addressed as 'young lady' was at least twenty years older than she.

'No pushing! No pushing!' another woman yelled, wedging her way through the line.

It was hopeless. The room was so packed, if anyone moved an elbow or tried to scratch a nose or an ear, everyone was jostled.

'Akh! Bozhe moi – my lord!' another old lady groaned as the man next to her tried to blow his nose.

Just then, a tall man in a black suit and a red tie stepped into the room. A handsome man with blond hair and blue eyes followed.

'Get in line!' somebody yelled.

'Where's the end of the line?' the man in the black suit asked politely.

'There, dummy!'

'Not there, stupid!' yelled the woman behind the place where the first lady had pointed. 'There!' she wagged her finger behind her. 'I was here first.'

'No, I was here first!'

'Well, I was here yesterday!'

'Well, I've been here for two years!'

'Not there!' a man yelled. 'There!' He too pointed behind him.

'Who is the last person?' the newly arrived person asked. No one replied. Everyone pointed at someone else.

'Well, this can't be a line then, if there's no end. Who's first?'

'I am!' a dozen people responded.

'This is truly no line, comrades!' said the man in the black suit, grinning. 'No end, and a dozen beginnings!'

'I was here before you!' A woman hit a man in the face with her purse.

'And I was here before you!' A man got whacked with a net bag filled with fish.

'The devil with you all! I was here first!' yelled a man with no teeth. He got a sack of turnips in the face for his trouble.

'Go ahead, Arnold! Try it,' said the man in the black suit to the man who'd followed him into the room.

Just then, the lightbulb hanging from a long, frayed cord over the clerk dimmed, then turned brighter. Murvella Petrovna squinted at her *Pravda*, and brought it closer towards her face. A loud buzzing filled the room. Then the old grease-caked black fan started to vibrate. Soon it was shaking all over, sliding up and down, across the crooked counter top.

'What the devil?' Murvella Petrovna asked, looking up from her paper.

'Precisely!' the blond man said so softly hardly anyone heard.

There was a grinding noise. The lightbulb dimmed again, swinging back and forth on its twisted cord. Then the fan blades started to turn, slowly, groaning. Then faster and faster. Soon the fan lifted right off the counter, hovering about a metre overhead.

'What the –?'

'— The devil!' someone shouted, completing the sentence.

Men ducked. Ladies grabbed on to their scarfs as the fan blades spun faster and faster. The fan hung suspended in air, its face now pointing menacingly towards Murvella Petrovna. Pages of *Pravda* blew out of the frightened clerk's hands and ended pasted flat up against the wall. A wind like a cyclone blew across the room. The supplicants ducked for cover. Murvella Petrovna ran and hid in a corner, peering out from behind a filing cabinet.

A sheet of paper lifted off from a stack of files on a desk, like a single bird in flight. Then another. Then a third. Then like a whole flock of birds scared by a rifle shot. Cardboard folders shuddered, and papers flew about the room. A bureaucratic blizzard. Visa permits. Receipts. Exit passport applications. Receipts for bribes, written in code. Ladies screamed. Men cursed. Everyone ducked.

'No challenge, Arnold. No challenge any more. Their technology makes it all too easy,' said the man in the black suit as he walked towards the door. His smiling blond companion followed.

Sixty-eight

'Chert poberi – the devil take it!' said the clerks as they worked late into the night, piecing back together their paper world. By the end of the third night, they'd only worked through the 'g's.

'Chert poberi!' said Murvella Petrovna, the chief clerk. 'Such disorder I've never seen! Chert! Chert! Chert!'

On Friday evening, she put the last piece of paper back into its proper file. It belonged in the 'p's. An exit application for Proplavskaya, Sonya Borisovna. It lay on the floor, under one leg of a three-legged stool. On top of it lay the official 'approved' stamp, inked side down. It had smeared across the application. Not quite in the right spot. But almost. 'Close enough,' Murvella Petrovna mumbled to herself. 'Chert! What disorder!'

Murvella placed this last piece of paper in the 'approval' stack, turned out the light, kicked the fan in the grid, and went to her drunken boyfriend.

Sixty-nine

'Good lad! Good lad!' The professor read over the first chapter. 'That's it, my little goose! Make it a story no one will put down!'

'Make them sad that it's over when it's over,' added Sofinya, her arm resting on the professor's arm.

When Ivanushka was done for the evening, the professor turned off the lamp glowing on Sofinya's desk.

The professor and Sofinya strolled down Bashmakovsky Street, arm in arm, and Ivanushka waddled close behind.

'Come, our little scribe!' Sofinya said. 'When you get tired, we'll carry you.'

The days were getting longer, and buds were starting to sprout on the linden trees. They were already selling kvass from barrels on the street corners.

Seventy

'Damned Russian heat!' Jennie Fliffle, the embassy clerk, hated Moscow. 'I wanted another embassy when I signed up,' she told her boss, Ambassador Rob Blavingworth.

'We're all stuck here, for now,' Mr Blavingworth told her. 'I studied German. I wanted Austria.'

'Any embassy but this one!' Jennie pleaded. 'I'd even take Canada!'

'You'd hate it there. Everyone says "doot" for "doubt" and "aboot" for "about".'

'But I studied French! I wanted to work in Paris!' she moaned. 'Here I am, stuck in this hell! Russian! Yuck! All those fat, ugly letters! Yuck!'

'Do well here, young lady, and soon you can request a transfer.'

'It won't be soon enough!' she replied, stomping off to her work station.

Her day was not going well. The computer room on the second floor of the American embassy was hot. The blowers weren't working. The air conditioning wasn't working. All those megabytes bouncing around made the room hotter.

'Their KGB is probably cooking us with microwaves from across the street besides!' Stanley Dafferdurv, her boss, whined. He too was in a bad mood. 'It's this damned Russian heat! The awful humidity! Look, my shirt's all wrinkled up already!' He pointed to the crease slowly disappearing along his shirt sleeve. 'So early in spring! Damnation! The computers have been acting up all day too,' he added, dusting off his terminal.

Poof! An orangeish powder filled the room. The lights

blinked. The green oval screens blinked too. Bright. Then dim. Then bright again. Then blank. The room turned dark.

'Shit! Shit! Shit!' It was Stanley's voice coming from somewhere in the smoky darkness. 'Turn off the computers! It's a surge! It'll ruin the data banks!'

Jennie fiddled for the dials and knobs her training had taught her to handle in daylight. It didn't work. 'Shit!' she yelled. 'There's no power! We can't turn them off! We need power to turn them off!'

The computer screens blinked on and off, and the magnetic discs whirred and stopped, whirred, span and stopped.

'Save! Save! Save the data!' Stanley's voice echoed inside the darkened room.

The computers were down now. Kaputsky. Not only were they down in Moscow, but the data bank in Washington was affected too. The surge had carried through the modems and across the lines. World War Three could have broken out right outside on Kalinin Prospekt. The whole world would know about it before the American embassy in Moscow knew anything. Shit!

Seventy-one

The lights and power were out in the computer room on the second floor, but things were more or less normal in the rest of the embassy. As normal, or abnormal, as they ever are. Soviet citizens clamouring to get in, begging for a look at a real drinking-fountain, the only one in the Soviet Union. Another crisis in the basement. The snack bar was out of Coca-Cola again. They'd have to buy that god-awful-tasting kvass from the natives again.

'Why thank you, Herr Professor Woland!' said Michael Fafferton, the attaché, sincerely. He shook the man's long hand warmly. 'Thank you. Your suggestions are wonderful! Imagine! A scientific exchange on parapsychological phenomena!'

'It could be of interest to all!' said Herr Professor Woland, nodding towards his dark-haired, square-shouldered assistant.

'Yes! Yes!' said Mr Fafferton warmly. 'And to think! You're a German! Bringing Russians and Americans together – how very touching! You must visit me in Sausilito sometimes!'

'That we will. That we will,' said the eminent professor. 'Come, Doctor Vasenka, let us repair to our research!'

The herr professor and his handsome assistant glanced into the darkened computer room as they passed.

'Hardly a challenge any more,' Woland said to his companion as he took his walking-stick and top hat from the garderobe attendant and headed for the exit.

Seventy-two

As Herr Woland stepped out on to Kalinin Prospekt, the lights throughout the embassy blinked. Whistles blew and bells rang. Marines jumped to attention at the gate, bayonets drawn. A German shepherd barked.

The lights in the computer room blinked too. Once. Then twice. Then they came on brighter than before. Then normal.

'Save now! Save! Save!' Stanley Dafferdurv shouted. Jennie complied, leaping from terminal to terminal. The discs span, and the daisy wheels inside the printers whirred.

Within a half hour, things were back to normal in the computer room. Back to as normal as they ever were, that is.

Jennie sat at her terminal, wiping the perspiration from her face. 'Damn heat! Damn chair too! Hurts my butt!' She squirmed as she bent forward, squinting into the monitor, chewing her gum loudly.

On her screen was the file name 'Thompson, Mary'. 'Attorney', it said. 'Assigned to Leningrad. Foreign Trade Office. Copyright negotiations. Security risk: none. Security clearance: none. Request to remain: granted.'

'Hmmm,' said Jennifer, chewing her gum. 'I thought I was still on the "p"s.'

She moved on to the 'u's and the 'v's before stepping down to the snack bar for another packet of bubblegum.

Seventy-three

Arnold looked back towards the spinning planet suspended in the distance, shrinking as the three steeds charged forward and upward. 'It's all that spinning around that makes things crazy.'

'You'd think they'd have got used to it by now,' said Vasenka, his black stallion keeping pace with Arnold's.

Ahead, Woland's steed reared its head and slowed, picking up speed again when Arnold and Vasenka caught up. 'The world,' Woland said, his head nodding backwards. 'It's always the same, yet always different.'

'About our friends,' said Arnold, his horse coming alongside Woland's. 'The professor – will he be all right? Will things go well for him?'

'Things always work out for the better,' Woland answered. 'Don't worry, friend. The professor will have happiness in his twilight years – happiness as he's never known.'

'With Sofinya?'

'Yes. And she shall have happiness too – much of it. They both deserve it.'

'And the professor's daughter?' Vasenka asked. 'And Sofinya's son, the poet?'

'They too shall have happiness. Mary and Misha. Sonya and David. They are the hope of the future.'

With that, Woland pulled in on his reins. His horse's head reared and headed upward, ever upward. 'All will be rewarded, in the proper way,' Woland said.

'And Ivanushka?' Arnold asked.

'He will write his tale. All of it. He's doing quite well.'

'What about the parts he doesn't know?' asked Vasenka.

'Those parts will come to him – we'll see to it. In his little goose dreams.'

'I'm pleased,' said Arnold. 'Everyone will be rewarded with comfort and peace.'

'Not with comfort. Not with peace,' Woland answered. 'With happiness.'

'What do you mean by "happiness" then – pleasure?'

Woland grinned, sitting high atop his steed. 'Languages have trouble with that idea – happiness.'

Arnold and Vasenka nodded.

'People have trouble too,' Woland added.

'What, then, would you call happiness?' asked Vasenka.

'Knowing you're doing something. Knowing that it changes things, even if just a little. That's happiness.'

'And what about all the others?' Arnold asked. 'Lydia Ivanovna. Flaffanoff. Bitonich. Durfdovich. The premier. What about them?'

'This is their punishment: their lives will remain as they are, as they've constructed them. That's punishment enough, my friends!'

Seventy-four

Woland pressed his knees into the side of the stallion, and the horse lunged forward, veering to the right, thirsty for movement, for speed. Vasenka and Arnold followed.

'You are my special assistants – you two – Russian and American,' Woland told them. 'Your former countries – they've created a lot of headaches. We'll work on them. All four of us.'

'All four of us?' asked Vasenka.

'Ivanushka will join us, when his work is finished.'

Vasenka and Arnold smiled.

Speeding past the moon, a cool but pleasant glow, metallic almost, settled on the sleek backs of the horses and on the robes of the riders. It was a windless, quiet, fleeting passage. The earth, now a small ball cast in dark blue, was wrapped in a swirl of white streaks of cloud.

It almost looked peaceful. There. Suspended. In heaven's darkness. With other spinning globes, suspended in the quiet night.

Seventy-five

By the time the new five-year plan came out (it was two years late in coming), it had become clear that Moscow had too many research institutes. The Tikvin Institute on Bashmakovsky Street was the first one on everybody's list for closing.

The Moscow City Soviet allowed the professor's laboratory to remain on the third floor. The space wouldn't be needed in the new plan.

Except for that, everything changed at Number Thirty-four Bashmakovsky Street. The name Tikvin fell into the ash can of history. The word was rubbed out of the stone arch over the doorway, and was crossed out on stationery. Even the garbage cans were painted over.

They hung a new plaque over the old one at the courtyard entrance. 'Heavenly Delight Pirozhki Factory'. The elevator still didn't work.

Comrade Petrushenko was appointed Heavenly Delight's security chief. It was his job to make sure that assembly-line workers didn't stuff meat or cabbage fillings into their purses or briefcases. (All Moscow's workers had taken up the habit of carrying briefcases. It made them look important, they thought, and the bulky cases worked well for stuffing lunches, lightbulbs stolen from offices, and fish from the corner market. Since all Muscovites now carried briefcases, it lost its status symbol. The question became, how does your briefcase smell? Only intellectuals had briefcases that didn't reek of fish and sausage.)

It was also Petrushenko's job to make sure workers didn't eat on the job, so he hung 'No eating!' signs all over the factory. There was one exception to the 'no eating rule'. Lydia Ivanovna, the factory's chief quality-control inspector, was allowed – encouraged, in fact – to eat all she wanted.

'Not enough grease in that one!' she'd yell, chomping between syllables.

'Too much dough in that one!'

'More filling!'

'Chomp!'

'Don't talk with your mouth full!' commanded Nikita, Head, Sanitation and Cleanliness.

Seventy-six

Comrade Hlafdarvich, Manager and Chief, Heavenly Delight Pirozhki Factory Workers' Cadre, decided that bugging pirozhki was an ideal way for the KGB to keep its fingers on the pulse of the city.

Comrade Flaffanoff, Head, Heavenly Delight Dough-forming Brigade, agreed. He put down his protractor, micrometer and drawings, and enlisted the help of Comrade Bitonich, wrapping-section head, to design a miniature microphone.

In three weeks, Bitonich reached his little hand up to the assembly line and plopped down something the size of a healthy collective-farm bedbug. He'd come up with a microphone smaller than an ordinary piece of gristle. Soviet gristle. Not Western gristle.

Moscow now lay open like the innards of a flayed fish.

Seventy-seven

'Chomp. Chomp. Chew. Hey, Vanya! Chomp. Chomp. I need a fuel pump for a 1936 Moskvitch!'

'You're out of luck, Tolya. The first ones were defective. Chomp. Those people are still waiting for their replacements!'

'You can help me, my friend? Chomp. You work in Fuel Pump Factory Number Seventeen?'

'Why yes. Chomp. I work there. I scrape the labels off imports. What's that in your hand? A side of beef?'

'Yes! Top quality too! Chomp. None of that collective-farm shit!'

'Where did you get it? Chomp.'

'Two nylon slips my wife stole off the assembly line. Chomp.'

'Where?'

'People's Intimates Factory Number Fifty-seven. Attached to the barbed-wire plant.'

Seventy-eight

The listening-devices worked well until they were swallowed. Then, unfortunately, came only gurgles and rumbles. Disgusting.

Seventy-nine

In similar fashion, six pairs of stolen nylon stockings and two pairs of panties were traced from Moscow Burlap Factory Number Seven to the mistress of a university professor, who himself had traded four hours of algebra tutoring for one pair of capitalist jeans with a red label on the back pocket.

'I threw in an eighth-century Russian icon too, Anniutochka, khe, khe, khe,' the professor told his mistress as he chomped on a cabbage-filled pirozhok during their stroll around Sparrow Hills.

'An eighth-century Russian icon?' Anniutochka asked. 'But Russia wasn't converted to Christianity until 988!'

'The dumb tourist didn't know that,' the professor replied. 'Here, sweetie, give me a bite of your pirozhok.'

'Chomp. Chomp. Gurgle. Rumble.'

Eighty

Within a half-hour, the bewildered professor and Anniutochka, his chubby mistress, stood in the people's criminals' interrogation box in the downtown Moscow precinct. Next to Anniutochka stood, equally bewildered, a worker with dirty hands clutching a fuel pump, and another worker holding on to a lean side of beef.

Eighty-one

It turned out that Heavenly Delight pirozhki were favourites with tourists. Stalls, stands and pirozhki kiosks popped up around all the foreigners' hotels. The Ukraina near the river. The Intourist on Gorky Street. The old Metropol near the Bolshoi.

A shiny new 'Pirozhki Bar' was installed next to the dollar store in the lobby of the Rossiya Hotel near the Kremlin. 'Please to be eatink and lovink good Russian meat pies!' proclaimed the banner hanging low across the lobby.

The tourists had trouble ordering, however. Selecting the proper filling. (There were two choices – cabbage, and meat and cabbage. There was more cabbage in the meat-and-cabbage combination, and about the same amount of meat in both.) Tourists invariably have trouble figuring out the subtleties of Soviet life.

Requesting greasy or extra-greasy – even that presented problems. Free samples, of course, were not permitted. That would have thrown off the productivity statistics.

Worse, getting currency from the tight-fisted foreigners was a problem. The dumb tourists stood around, staring at the kopecks lying in their palms as if the coins were a rash. German tourists mumbled. The French nodded cynically, pointing with disdain at grease spots on the wrapping-paper. Italians hardly gestured, and Americans hardly bought. It had become clear to the nomenklatura – the hierarchy of the Bureau for Tourists' Sustenance in the Physical Spheres – that help of the first order of quality was needed.

A call went out for bilingual or trilingual pirozhki vendors. Comrade Durfdovich got himself a new job.

Eighty-two

'Hey, good buddy! Give me one of them thar greasy things!' said an Amerikan in a wide-brimmed hat with a smile that was wider. He was standing outside the Metropol Hotel. A group of visiting collective-farm workers gathered around him to stare at his hat and his pointed boots.

'Kheer you are, goood ser!' said Durfdovich, ducking. Prior experience had taught him to duck when dealing with Amerikans.

Durfdovich liked his new job. Hardly anyone ever punched him.

Eighty-three

It turned out that the Prezident of Amerika had grown fond of pirozhki during his short stay in Moscow. The great comrade premier started sending him daily supplies.

'Chomp. Chomp. Fucking reporters!' The words came by surveillance satellite all the way from the prezident's breakfast table, right into KGB headquarters near Dzerzhinsky Square. 'Chomp. Chomp. Fucking press! I'd like to lock all the bastards up! Kill 'em!'

'Now, now dear! Calm down. You'll ruin your digestion.'

'Fuck 'em anyway! The god-damned senate too!'

'Remember your stitches, dear. The doctor told you not to get worked up.'

'Nuke 'em! Nuke everybody!'

Eighty-four

In return for the pirozhki, the Amerikan Prezident started sending the great comrade an Amerikan delicacy. It seemed to be a delicacy, that is. A black, cylindrical fluffy thing with a white gooey paste in the centre. A swirl of the same white goo spread across the top in a curlicue.

The KGB ordered a complete analysis, and decided it was a secret script for hidden informers. When it was decided that the thing was not poison (nor of any nutritional merit), the premier, after much pleading with the minister of security, was allowed to eat the delicacies.

'Hmpfff,' said his regal shortness. The wrapping,

though attractive, did not taste good. The contents tasted about the same. The KGB did another analysis. Man-made ingredients. Probably not food. Paraphenyl-carogeenics. Guar gum. Tofu. It sounded like the cast of a Hindu movie. No vitamins. No minerals. Not even roughage.

But alas! Those clever Amerikans had come up with a listening-device made out of a pliant, creamy substance, no bigger than a speck. Harder to find than flyshit in pepper.

'Comrade Bitonich!' the great one bellowed at the trembling little man three months later. 'Make one smaller than this!' he commanded, holding a white speck with a pair of tiny tweezers. 'Or your days in Heavenly Delight are numbered! I'll send you to Hell's Bells, in Manchuria!'

Eighty-five

Petrushenko did a good job with security at the Heavenly Bliss Pirozhki Factory. All his listening-devices from the former Tikvin Institute, now in the ash can of history, remained in place. Bitonich's new sub-miniature microphones helped too.

The factory's regimen was strict. If a worker sat too long on the toilet, a voice boomed out of the walls, 'Comrade, shame on you! Shirking! Not shitting!'

'But I am! I am!' was the usual plaintive reply.

'Two minutes squatting there! And not one plop? Not a tinkle! Come now, comrade! Zip up and get back to work!'

Eighty-six

The demand for Heavenly Bliss pirozhki rose, so quotas were raised too. Flaffanoff, Bitonich, Lydia Ivanovna, Petrushenko – they all got raises and bonuses. Nikita, Head, Sanitation and Cleanliness, got a new broom, with a long handle even, on the provision that he stop complaining about flour droppings, and stop calling Lydia Ivanovna a dirigible.

Durfdovich sold more pirozhki than anyone else, despite the fact that he spent three weeks in the hospital recovering from a whiplash. A man from Texas had slapped him kindly on the back. The ever-apprehensive Durfdovich mistook the man's motives, ducked too quickly, slipped, and fell into a vat of lard.

The Heavenly Bliss Pirozhki Factory always filled its quota. Over-fulfilled, if the truth be told. It was even on an evening Radio Moscow broadcast.

And through it all, Lydia Ivanovna had the last word.

'Not greasy enough!'

'Not enough dough!'

'More filling!'

No. Nikita had the last word. 'Stop talking with your mouth full, you blimp!'

Eighty-seven

The elevator in the Heavenly Bliss Pirozhki Factory didn't work, just as the elevator in the Tikvin Research Institute hadn't worked.

The premier himself wrote a formal letter of complaint to the French premier, to be sent by diplomatic pouch. Durfdovich was called in on special assignment to handle the translating.

Dear Manure-Head Premier:

Vat is beeg idea of elevator sellink us for big and hard Western currency not working never, turd? So you Frenchman can notink do right except eatink leever pate?

We not buyink Pierre Cardin jeansy den! Unless you make elevator workink, up and down too! Not stoppink!

Two months you got! Den we buy Levi's!

Eighty-eight

'We're so proud, Ivanushka!' Sofinya exclaimed as she leaned over the black Smit-Korona. 'You've almost finished!'

'My beak hurts and I'm tired!'

'Come, my little one. Let's all of us go for a walk,' said the professor.

They walked out into the cool fall air.

'I can't wait until I'm transformed! Then I'll walk faster than you!' said Ivanushka, waddling and struggling to take up the rear.

'When you've finished, my feathered companion, you will be higher and faster than we,' said Sofinya.

They slowed down to the goose's pace.

'How excited I am for you!' she told the professor as she took his arm. 'Imagine! Your daughter visiting. Her husband too! All the way from Kalifornia-Amerika!'

'Yes, my dearest. And soon, Misha and his Mary! Right

here in Moscow for a month's visit. And a whole new volume of poems to read! How wonderful!'

The elderly couple walked arm in arm down kinky Bashmakovsky Street, crooked old buildings turning every which way. Behind the couple, complaining but ever so softly, waddled Ivanushka.